"What are you doing in the woods this time of night?" *Lexi asked.*

"Making sure you get home okay. It can't be safe out here." Brett's gaze snagged on her mouth and held there so long her lips parted.

She wanted him to kiss her. Her brain screamed a warning, but her body didn't listen. Grabbing the front of his shirt, she pulled him closer. "But who's going to keep *you* safe?"

On either side of her head his hands pressed tight against the tree at her back. Beneath her fist his heart hammered.

Lexi leaned forward and, with a low rumble that echoed through his chest, Brett devoured her.

She'd expected him to be cool and calculating. Instead, his mouth was hot and demanding. Need wrapped around her, clenching deep inside.

Finally, he broke away. They stared at each other. Never had a single kiss left her so shaken.

What had she been thinking? She'd worked so hard to learn impulse control. Tonight those lessons had failed her...in the most delicious way....

Dear Reader,

Just like Lexi, one of my weaknesses is chocolate. Anyone who follows me on Twitter or Facebook already knows that each of my books is fueled by a different kind of candy. For *She's No Angel,* it was Dove milk chocolates. You know you've indulged a lot when just the sight of that blue-and-silver bag makes your blood sugar spike. But they were so yummy and every calorie was worth it.

Aside from my love of anything sweet and gooey, I also wanted to mention Little Bits, Lexi's shy and skittish cat. Little Bits is based on a real cat available for adoption from www.safeplacepets.org. This organization finds forever homes for pets with terminally ill owners. I was drawn to Little Bits the moment I saw her picture. A little pudgy, just like Lexi used to be, she isn't perfect...but she's absolutely perfect for Lexi. If you're considering a furry companion, don't overlook your local shelter. My family is so much richer thanks to Captain Jack and Savannah, the cat and dog we've adopted.

Check out the Blaze Authors' Pet Project at blazeauthors.com for more details.

I'm so excited to share Lexi and Brett's story with you and hope you enjoy it! I love to hear from my readers at kira@kirasinclair.com, or drop me a note at P.O. Box 5083, Decatur, AL 35601.

Best Wishes,

Kira

She's No Angel

—

Kira Sinclair

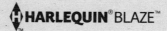
HARLEQUIN® BLAZE™

If you purchased this book without a cover you should be aware that this book is stolen property. It was reported as "unsold and destroyed" to the publisher, and neither the author nor the publisher has received any payment for this "stripped book."

Recycling programs
for this product may
not exist in your area.

ISBN-13: 978-0-373-79762-2

SHE'S NO ANGEL

Copyright © 2013 by Kira Bazzel

All rights reserved. Except for use in any review, the reproduction or utilization of this work in whole or in part in any form by any electronic, mechanical or other means, now known or hereafter invented, including xerography, photocopying and recording, or in any information storage or retrieval system, is forbidden without the written permission of the publisher, Harlequin Enterprises Limited, 225 Duncan Mill Road, Don Mills, Ontario, Canada M3B 3K9.

This is a work of fiction. Names, characters, places and incidents are either the product of the author's imagination or are used fictitiously, and any resemblance to actual persons, living or dead, business establishments, events or locales is entirely coincidental.

This edition published by arrangement with Harlequin Books S.A.

For questions and comments about the quality of this book, please contact us at CustomerService@Harlequin.com.

® and TM are trademarks of Harlequin Enterprises Limited or its corporate affiliates. Trademarks indicated with ® are registered in the United States Patent and Trademark Office, the Canadian Trade Marks Office and in other countries.

Printed in U.S.A.

ABOUT THE AUTHOR

Kira Sinclair is an award-winning author who writes emotional, passionate contemporary romances. Double winner of the National Readers' Choice Award, her first foray into writing fiction was for a high-school English assignment. Nothing could dampen her enthusiasm...not even being forced to read the love story aloud to the class. However, it definitely made her blush. Writing about striking, sexy heroes and passionate, determined women has always excited her. She lives out her own *happily ever after* with her amazing husband, their two beautiful daughters and a menagerie of animals on a small farm in North Alabama. Kira loves to hear from readers at www.KiraSinclair.com.

Books by Kira Sinclair

HARLEQUIN BLAZE

415—WHISPERS IN THE DARK
469—AFTERBURN
588—CAUGHT OFF GUARD
605—WHAT MIGHT HAVE BEEN
667—BRING IT ON*
672—TAKE IT DOWN*
680—RUB IT IN*
729—THE RISK-TAKER

*Island Nights

To get the inside scoop on Harlequin Blaze and its talented writers, be sure to check out blazeauthors.com.

Other titles by this author available in ebook format.
Don't miss any of our special offers. Write to us at the following address for information on our newest releases.

Harlequin Reader Service
U.S.: 3010 Walden Ave., P.O. Box 1325, Buffalo, NY 14269
Canadian: P.O. Box 609, Fort Erie, Ont. L2A 5X3

This book is for my fabulous agent, Lucienne Diver. Your insight, honesty and support mean more than you know. Somehow you instinctively sense when I need an ego boost, a reminder to get back on track or just a quiet voice saying I can do this. Thanks for believing in me!

1

CHOCOLATE WAS Lexi Harper's drug of choice. The only thing that could beat the decadent taste of that melted goodness was really stellar sex. Unfortunately, her hips proved that chocolate—even the gourmet stuff—was easier to come by.

Which is probably why she'd opened her own shop. There was something about baked goods that made everyone happy. You couldn't frown with a piece of fudge in your mouth. It was physically impossible.

Well, for everyone except Mrs. Copeland, who could frown no matter what.

"Alexis Harper!"

Sighing, Lexi suppressed a cringe and turned to look at the self-appointed grande dame of Sweetheart, South Carolina.

"I'll be with you in just a moment, Mrs. Copeland," Lexi said in her sweetest voice. Even if it killed her she'd be nice.

Mrs. Copeland pinned Lexi beneath a steely glare that was specifically designed to have her spine snapping straight and Lexi jumping to do her bidding. She was intimately acquainted with the look and had been since the age of ten.

"I've been waiting here for almost fifteen minutes," she barked.

Old habits were hard to break and a residual shudder ran down Lexi's spine. While she was growing up, Mrs. Copeland had been her etiquette instructor. On the third Saturday of every month for eight years, Lexi's mother would ship her off for several dreadful hours where the woman delighted in pointing out every flaw, gaffe or perceived slight.

Who really needed to know the proper way to pour tea or where to sit the governor if he should happen to agree to dinner? Lexi had certainly never run across the need for most of the things that Mrs. Copeland viewed as more important than breathing. And what little she had used would have been covered by human decency and politeness.

After one particularly embarrassing incident involving mustard, a Siamese cat and licorice when she was twelve, Lexi had begged her mom not to send her back. But there were certain things that happened in Sweetheart, and attending Mrs. Copeland's etiquette classes was one of them. Along with the debutante ball.

Just the thought of it sent another shiver of remembered dread down Lexi's spine. God, she'd been such a spastic klutz back then.

"Everyone else has been waiting just as long, Mrs. Copeland. Longer, since they were here before you."

Off to her left, in front of the caramel apple display, Mary Beth Hereford snickered. Lexi didn't know Mary

Beth well, but despite that, the two of them shared a knowing glance that immediately bonded them.

Mrs. Copeland's mouth tightened into a hard, unpleasant line. She didn't say anything else, but the unpleasant knot in the pit of Lexi's stomach didn't ease. And it wouldn't until the horrid witch left. Lexi wanted to hate herself for letting the woman get under her skin. Mrs. Copeland couldn't hurt or embarrass her anymore. But logic apparently couldn't trump remembered misery and years of ingrained dread.

Pushing the unpleasantness aside, Lexi focused on the rest of her customers. She cut and boxed a set of chocolate-dipped, rum-soaked caramel apples for Mary Beth. She was hosting Bunco, a dice game, tonight. Mr. Arcella had stopped in for a box of assorted truffles for his wife. It was their twenty-fourth anniversary. Lexi slipped in several of Mrs. Arcella's favorite flavor— champagne—even though he didn't ask for them.

She spent another five minutes answering the questions of a woman she didn't recognize. The woman wanted to know about Lexi's herb-infused aphrodisiac chocolates, which probably meant she was from out of town. The best thing Lexi had ever done was start advertising those on the internet. Customers had been coming out of the woodwork ever since.

The line finally cleared and Mrs. Copeland was up. Turning to the woman, Lexi braced herself for whatever unpleasantness was coming—because it always did. The woman viewed it as her personal crusade to point out everyone else's flaws while simultaneously breaking as many of her precious etiquette rules as humanly possible.

She didn't disappoint. "Aphrodisiac chocolates. That's disgraceful, Alexis Harper."

Lexi bit her tongue and swallowed the automatic response at not only the woman's acerbic tone but at the use of her given name. No one, not even her own mother, called her Alexis anymore. But Mrs. Copeland despised nicknames.

"Heaven only knows what your poor mama thinks about those…" She waved her hand at the artfully sensual display beneath the glass. "…those things."

"Why don't you ask her, Mrs. Copeland?" Lexi suggested, a calm, fake smile curling her lips. She folded her hands on the glass countertop and leaned across as if she were imparting a secret. "Better yet, why don't you ask Daddy at the council meeting tomorrow night? Mama took some home just last week."

Mrs. Copeland's eyes widened and then narrowed dangerously. "Well," she huffed. "I shouldn't be surprised. You always were a hopeless cause, Alexis Harper. My one true disappointment as an educator."

If Mrs. Copeland was an educator then Lexi was a supermodel, something that was so far from the realm of possibility as to be pure fairy tale.

Lexi boxed Mrs. Copeland's selection of iced petit fours and, though it galled her, decorated the thing with her signature red gingham bow.

"At least you've found a way to make a living from your love of sugar," Mrs. Copeland offered with a sharp smirk. "Although I never would have expected you to slim down nearly as much with all this temptation around. Bless your heart, there wasn't a Saturday you came into my class that you didn't have a smear of chocolate somewhere, was there?"

Lexi gritted her teeth and jerked her mouth up into the approximation of a smile. And hoped her eyes weren't glaring daggers the way she feared.

"Yes, ma'am. I'm real lucky."

"Good breeding helps," Mrs. Copeland offered as a parting salvo with a glance up and down that left the unmistakable impression of her opinion. Apparently, in Lexi's case, good breeding wasn't quite enough. Although the old biddy's opinion wasn't exactly a news flash.

When the bell tinkled and the door snicked shut, Lexi slumped tiredly against the edge of the display case. A few moments. That's all she needed, and then she could handle closing up the shop.

"Why didn't you put her in her place?"

The low, smoky voice startled Lexi, and she jerked her spine straight again.

A man she'd never met stood in the far corner leaning against her shelf of prebagged goodies. She'd been so preoccupied that she hadn't noticed him.

"Because it would have been wasted breath, and I try not to waste anything."

His arms were crossed negligently over a wide chest. The line of his body stretched out, long and tempting. Tight jeans clung to thick thighs and Lexi had no doubt that if he turned around she'd get a nice view of a high, round rear. Her body reacted immediately, coming alive at the presence of a virile male in the center of her world. She clamped down on the buzz of female interest.

He was a stranger, and after what had happened a few months ago, she didn't trust strangers.

He studied her with cool blue eyes that had another knot of unease forming in her belly. Lexi didn't like being watched. Nothing good had ever come from being the center of attention. As the mayor's daughter, everyone in town knew her and thought her life was fair game for comment. The perils of living in a small town.

For a long time she'd struggled to figure out who she was. There were so many loud voices in her head telling her what she should do, how she should feel and what she should be. Finding a place where everyone else's opinion of her didn't matter had been a hard battle.

She was happy with the life she'd built. She had a good business, wonderful friends and she'd come to terms with her own weaknesses. Most days she was good, although every now and then old ghosts resurfaced.

His scrutiny made her uncomfortable. And warm. He straightened and stalked across her shop with a predatory grace that left her mouth dry as cotton. All bunching muscles and laser focus. He smiled and her stomach tightened.

She didn't want to notice the way his bottom lip pulled up in the center. Or the brush of dark brown hair that touched the curve of his ears. She didn't want to notice him at all.

Breaking the hold he had on her, Lexi dropped her gaze and fiddled with the boxes beneath the display counter. Stacking and restacking them, despite the fact that they were already perfectly straight.

"What's good?"

"Everything," she answered without pause. Every single thing in the ten-foot-long case had been handmade. By her. And since quality control was a major concern, she'd personally sampled everything. Once and only once. Followed immediately by at least five miles on the treadmill currently sitting idle in the office at the back of her store.

It was either that or go back to being "Piglet" Harper. A prospect she did not relish. The nickname might have been cute when Gage, her brother, gave it to her as a baby, but right around middle school the charm had disappeared. Unfortunately, the name hadn't.

"I need something for dessert."

"Well…" Lexi's gaze swept the case. "For how many?"

"I have no idea."

"A challenge."

He leaned closer to the case. The scent of his aftershave, something clean, crisp and totally male, mixed with the tempting scent of sugar. Lexi's mouth began to water.

"Do you like challenges?" he asked, one eyebrow pulling up in a dare all its own.

He was flirting. The blood pounding furiously through her veins and the interested crackle beneath her skin told her that. But she wasn't going there.

Although somehow she found herself snapping back. "Nope, I like life easy and boring." Which really was the truth. She didn't like drama. She was perfectly content with the nice, quiet life she'd built for herself.

"I can tell." A smile rippled across his lips, but before it could fully form he pulled it back.

She had a great business she could be proud of,

good friends, and whenever she had an itch that needed scratching, a big city close enough to provide some pleasant diversion.

It was obvious this man had the skills to be very *diverting,* but after Brandon she'd learned to be cautious with men who walked through her front door.

With a deep breath Lexi broke away from whatever *this* was and focused on her job. "Well, you could take petit fours, but you don't strike me as a tiny bite of cake kinda guy."

"Uh, no. I don't like tiny bites of anything."

An unexpected shiver lanced through her. Lexi clenched her fists and ignored it.

"There's always caramel apples, but somehow those seem more intimate and since you don't know how many people are coming that probably won't work."

He shook his head.

All of the brownies and cakes she'd made today had sold hours ago. She did have one, a new recipe she'd tried and was planning to drop off to Gage and Hope, her best friend and future sister-in-law, on her way home. She hesitated to sell a product that she hadn't fully vetted, but she'd been perfecting the recipe for the lemon-cardamom cake for months and finally thought she'd gotten it right.

Besides, she didn't have anything else that would work, and she hated to send a customer away unhappy. Especially a new one. Okay, maybe she just didn't want to send *this* one away unhappy. But what was wrong with that? She was big on customer service.

Turning away, Lexi slipped through the curtain into the back. A few moments later she reemerged with a cake covered in rose-scented frosting and candied rose petals.

"Will this work?"

He straightened from the languid slouch against her counter and stared, wide-eyed, at the cake in her hands. The playful, watchful air he'd had disappeared. "That's too pretty to eat."

She'd surprised him. Which surprised her. And possibly pissed her off. What had he expected her to pull from the back? A chocolate cake with canned frosting slapped on top?

"Nonsense," she said, her voice tight with a suppressed frown. Lexi reached down for a box and a bow. "Food is meant to be enjoyed. Savored. Especially dessert."

She handed the box to him. "That'll be thirty-five." His fingers brushed against her hand. His cool blue eyes went from watchful to melting. A zap of electricity blasted up her arms and she almost dropped the cake.

He scrambled to rebalance the weight of it in his palms. "Well, it would have been a shame if something that pretty had hit the floor. Tasting this is about the only thing I'm looking forward to tonight."

Unbidden, a vision of him feeding her bites of that cake swelled in her mind. Her lungs labored to catch a breath, and she licked her lips. She hadn't meant to, but she'd wanted to taste that icing and the skin of his fingers beneath. The flavor of her own lips wasn't nearly as exciting.

His eyes snagged on her mouth. The box crackled in protest as his hands tightened, threatening to crush the cardboard.

The phone beneath the counter rang, breaking the spell.

Oh, Lord, what was she doing? This man was a complete stranger. A customer! He'd been in her store for less than fifteen minutes and her libido was ready to flip the open sign over and drag him into the back for a different kind of workout than her treadmill provided.

Turning her back, she answered the phone. "Sugar and Spice."

"Oh, thank goodness you're still there." Her mother's frazzled voice echoed down the line. "I need a huge favor."

The bell behind her chimed. Lexi turned to see who'd come into the store only to discover it was empty. And two twenties were on the counter.

She should be grateful that he was gone, but her energized body certainly wasn't happy. Tough. Dragging in a deep breath, Lexi held it for a moment before letting it—and the last fifteen minutes—go.

"Alexis Harper, are you listening to me?"

Shaking her head, Lexi refocused. "I'm sorry, Mama, I was distracted. What favor?"

"Please tell me you have something in the case I could use for dessert."

"I just sold my last cake."

"Dammit!"

Lexi straightened. Her mother never swore. This was obviously more than a rampant sweet tooth. "Don't worry, give me an hour and I can make something. What's this about?"

"I knew I could count on you, Lexi. Be sure to wear something nice."

"Uh, why?" She had an early morning tomorrow and had really just planned to head home, curl up with Little Bits, her cat, and watch mindless TV for a while before crashing into bed. The good thing about hand making all of her products was that she could guarantee quality. The bad thing was that, since she was an exacting perfectionist, she had to be up bright and early every morning to actually do the hand making.

"A representative from Bowen Enterprises showed up today. He's here for the council meeting tomorrow night. Your father invited the man to dinner."

That was her daddy all right. Friends close and enemies closer. There was a reason he'd been mayor of Sweetheart for the past eighteen years. He was smart, cunning and charming.

"I still don't understand what this has to do with me."

"I need you to balance out our numbers, dear. See you in an hour."

Without giving her a chance to protest, her mom hung up. For about sixty seconds Lexi thought about calling back and telling her no way. But although the idea held appeal, Lexi knew she wouldn't do it.

Instead, she headed back to the kitchen to evaluate what she had that could be thrown together in an hour. Whatever it was would have to be spectacular.

Everyone in town hated Bowen Enterprises and everything the company stood for. Several months ago they had submitted plans to build a monstrously tacky resort at the lake on the very edge of town.

The council had denied their request for rezoning and had refused to issue building permits.

Mr. Bowen had not been happy, but they hadn't heard anything from him in months.

Apparently, it was finally time for round two.

BRETT NEWCOMB SHOVED open the door to the only hotel in Sweetheart—if it could really be called that. Briarwood Inn was more of a glorified B and B. It was bigger than most B and Bs he'd stayed in, boasting twenty-some rooms instead of only a handful. But it clearly wasn't big enough to handle all the tourist traffic during Sweetheart's high season.

Which was why he was there. Sweetheart might not realize why they needed him—well, needed Bowen Enterprises, the company he worked for—but they would.

He had to admit, although a little reluctantly, the place had an old-world charm that somehow managed to match the town. The room was huge and homey. Welcoming in a way that most hotel rooms never quite managed to achieve. And he'd know. He'd been designing hotels and commercial buildings for the past six years.

The room was filled with mismatched furniture that looked well cared for, but also worn with age. The whole inn left guests feeling as though they were staying with long-lost relatives instead of in a room used by countless strangers.

And while that might appeal to some, what Bowen intended to give the area was a sensual oasis where lovers and honeymooners could luxuriate.

In the past twenty years, Sweetheart, South Carolina, had built a reputation for being a quaint, romantic getaway. After the local textile mill closed, a large portion of the residents, suddenly out of work, turned their energies to capitalizing on the marketing ploy that was their name. And they'd done well.

The Cupid Festival in February was a famous week-long celebration. During spring and summer the town park was booked with back-to-back weddings. The shops in the area specialized in high-end, personalized customer service.

Sweetheart gave visitors a glimpse into all the best things small-town life could provide. And when their trip was over guests went back to their Starbucks, take-out Chinese and the comfort of the rat race.

The problem was that the growing crowds were outstripping the town's capacity. Which is where he and Bowen stepped in—with an enormous resort facility that would include gourmet restaurants, spa services, state-of-the-art exercise facilities, pools and hot tubs. And if he secretly felt some of the details his boss wanted to include veered just this side of tacky, the plans were still a work in progress, and they had plenty of time to revise.

Brett tossed down his suitcases and gently placed the cake box with its gingham ribbon on the dresser. His fingers ran across the rough texture of the bow. It made him think about the matching apron the woman who sold it to him had been wearing.

Every muscle in his body tightened. She was beautiful and distracting. Illogically, he wanted to coax her out of all that red and white. Maybe his trip to Sweetheart wouldn't be all bad. He'd anticipated weeks of banging his head against a backwoods brick wall trying to convince the entire town that building a resort was a good idea.

This inn practically proved his point for him. The entire town was losing revenue, along with the rest of the businesses, although none of them seemed to notice or care. At least not yet. He intended to point it out. Maybe he'd start his campaign to win over the business owners with Sugar & Spice.

But not tonight. Tonight he had to concentrate on dinner with the mayor. Brett had been shocked at the invitation. He'd stopped at the Town Hall when he arrived, more as a courtesy than anything else. He'd requested time on the meeting agenda and been granted it. He had no idea what ulterior motives Mayor Harper was working, but knew they were there.

They always were.

The town needed the resort Bowen was proposing to build. And even if he had his own reservations about the project, he had a job to do.

And if he pulled this off, he'd get a generous bonus in the bargain. A bonus he desperately needed in order to break away from Bowen.

When Brett first started as an intern at Bowen almost ten years ago, he'd been impressed with the way his boss had managed to parlay his experience as a construction worker into being the head of a multimillion-dollar real estate empire.

It was the life Brett had always wanted. The kind of easy assurance he'd never known growing up.

It had taken scholarships, loans he was still paying off and two part-time jobs to get him through college. But he'd always known education was his best shot at a better life for himself, his mom and his little brother.

He'd wanted the life Mr. Bowen had—houses, cars, a

wife beautiful enough to grace glossy magazine pages. Security. He'd wanted the chance to repay his mother for all the sacrifices she'd ever made.

Then he'd gotten to know the guy.

Oh, Brett was all for smart business. Spending a dollar just to spend it was pointless. But there was a difference between frugality and knowingly purchasing inferior materials and cutting every corner possible. All with the intention of dumping the shoddy finished product on unsuspecting buyers long before the cracks started to show.

The problem was that his boss wasn't exactly doing anything illegal. Immoral? Sure. But there wasn't much he could do about it.

Except get out.

And he had a plan. A plan to open his own architecture firm. One where he could control what they did and how they did it. His mom could run the office. Hunter, his baby brother, who was about to graduate with a degree in electrical engineering, could help.

But that was easier said than done. The money it took to start a business was unbelievable. People expected a certain image when they hired a design team. These days it was sleek glass and expensive fixtures. High-end equipment. The insurance and bond estimates alone had almost given him a heart attack.

And Hunter still had another semester of college, which he was paying for. And his mom really needed a new car. Her old sedan, Francesca, was nine years old and had been in the shop seven times in the last year. He kept expecting the next phone call from the mechanic to be the death knell.

Every time he turned around something was eating a hole in the nest egg he'd been steadily building since the day he went to work. But with the bonus… It was just the large influx of cash he needed to push that magical number over the edge and allow him to go out on his own.

He'd use any means at his disposal to get the Sweetheart deal through. Nothing was going to stand in his way.

2

LEXI BALANCED THE crystal trifle bowl filled with the death-by-chocolate yumminess she'd thrown together. Hopping on one foot at a time, she slipped on the heels she'd borrowed from Willow and wished she had another hand to tug at the skirt of the dress she'd borrowed. It was a bit short, but thank God one of her best friends just happened to own a dress boutique and couture wedding gown business.

Popping down to Willow's store had saved her a lengthy trip home, although she'd wasted some of that time chatting with her friend. The simple black cocktail dress was a little over the top for dinner at her parents' but beggars couldn't be choosers. At least it didn't sport rhinestones. Lexi had vetoed anything that sparkled before Willow could even pull it from the rack.

The four-inch red heels were bad enough, but Willow had insisted. Something about a pop of color. Lexi didn't care about color. She cared about comfort and the damn things already hurt. But she couldn't very well wear her chocolate-spattered runners.

Turning around, she bumped the door to her SUV

closed with her rear. The curtain at the front window twitched, pulling her attention. Probably Mama waiting impatiently for her to arrive. She was only fifteen minutes late.

For Lexi, that was practically early.

She'd already started to juggle everything, trying to find an empty hand so that she could grasp the knob, when the side door flew open. "There you are, dear. I was beginning to worry." The hard look in her mother's eyes didn't match the fake smile on her lips.

Her mother had given up worrying when she was a little late a long time ago. She wasn't the child most likely to give her mother heart palpitations—that honor belonged to her brother, Gage, a daredevil former army ranger. Lexi was solid. She was good and quiet and did what she was told. And always had.

Without giving her a chance to rebalance everything, her mom swept her into the house. She pushed Lexi, not with her hands but with the frown on her face and her relentless forward movement.

"Mom, wait," Lexi tried to protest, but her mother wasn't listening.

The door slammed behind them. Her purse strap slid from its precarious position on her shoulder and slammed into the bend in her elbow. The bowl in her hands bobbled. The new shoes pinched and she wobbled. Lexi tried to grab for everything—equilibrium, trifle, kitchen counter.

She didn't have enough hands. Something was going. Unfortunately, it was the dessert.

The bowl crashed to the floor and splintered. Chocolate mousse, brownie pieces, whipped cream and crystal shards exploded everywhere.

Lexi caught herself on the counter, bent over, so she was staring straight at a pair of glossy black men's shoes covered in fudge sauce and pecan pieces. A single cherry rested on the left toe of the expensive leather.

Her mother moaned. Behind her she heard the sound of her father's smothered laughter.

Her gaze moved slowly up the length of crisp slacks that were now splattered with a combination of sticky substances that would probably never come out. Hell, there was fudge on his knee. Wide hands hung beside narrow hips. The dark gray dress shirt tucked into the waistband showed off broad shoulders.

Lexi swallowed and sighed inwardly. She should have known better than to wear heels like these. She was a walking disaster without adding inches between the soles of her feet and the ground.

But the automatic apology died on her lips when her gaze collided with cool, icy eyes. His mouth twitched.

"You," she breathed, because she couldn't think of anything else.

"Brett Newcomb, may I introduce my daughter, Lexi Harper," her father's voice drawled dryly from behind her.

She blinked and fought the urge to run screaming from the room. It was an old reaction. Her childhood response to these kind of embarrassing situations that seemed to follow her like the plague.

Snapping her jaw shut, she pushed away from the counter and straightened to her artificially enhanced height. The towel she grabbed from the kitchen counter snapped.

"I'm so sorry," she offered in a clear voice as she crouched by his feet to try and clean up some of the mess.

He followed her down, stilling her hands. "No worries." His dark voice rumbled through her. "But that is a terrible waste of chocolate."

His eyes glittered at her, like the tiny pieces of glass stuck in the mess on his shoes. He was laughing at her, although his mouth stayed in a perfectly straight line.

Lexi did not like being laughed at. She'd had enough of being the butt of other people's jokes growing up.

"Are you making fun of me?"

"Absolutely not." His mouth twitched. She didn't believe him. In a fit of temper, she uttered something nasty beneath her breath and threw the towel down at his feet.

"Alexis Harper…" Her mother's voice cracked out a warning.

Lexi regretted her reaction immediately. It was petty and the entire mess was her fault. But he'd unwittingly trampled all over a deep-seated hot-button issue.

"I'm so sorry, Brett." Her mom moved into damage-control mode. "Honey, can you get me the broom and dustpan?"

As she leaned down to clean up the mess, her mom started clucking. "Let me throw your pants and socks into the wash. I'm sure we can find you something to wear until they're clean."

Oh, crap. All she needed was for this man to be walking around half naked. Her body was already going haywire.

And he hadn't taken his eyes from her yet.

Heat suffused her, delayed embarrassment and something so much worse.

Brett grasped her mom's hands and stopped her fussing. "Be careful, Mrs. Harper, I don't want you to cut yourself. I'm fine. Nothing a damp cloth can't fix."

From his crouched position on the floor, he looked up at Lexi. A spark of heat flickered deep in the center of all that cool blue. "Guess it's a good thing I bought that cake, after all."

TO SAY THAT he'd been shocked to see the woman from Sugar & Spice alighting from the car in the Harpers' driveway would be an understatement. Well, the shock had mostly come from seeing her in a tiny black dress instead of the gingham apron.

The long blond hair she'd had pulled into a tight tail trailed invitingly down her back in a wave of curls. Watching her bounce from foot to foot as she'd pulled on her heels and tugged at her hem had surprised him. Watching a woman dress had never intrigued him before.

But she did. The little black dress was a glimpse of what lay beneath the peaches-and-cream complexion and sugar-cookie scent.

Without letting go of Mrs. Harper, Brett stood, bringing her with him. He smiled down at the woman. Dressed in conservative slacks, a purple silk top and a single strand of pearls, she reminded him of every sitcom mom. The kind of mother he'd never had.

He'd bet Mrs. Harper had been at home just waiting for the kids to hop off the bus in the afternoon. She'd greet them with warm cookies and a glass of milk and ask them how their day went.

Brett and Hunter had returned home to an empty house. The only time they'd gotten cookies was when the store brand had been on sale.

Shaking his head, Brett pushed the unexpected reaction away.

"I'm fine, Mrs. Harper. Really."

Taking the broom from Mr. Harper's hand, he began sweeping up the mess. It took him several moments before he realized the three other people were staring at him. A frown accompanied Lexi's narrowed brown gaze.

"What?"

"You're a guest in our home, Mr. Newcomb."

"Brett."

"Brett. Why are you cleaning up a mess you didn't make?"

He shrugged. "Because it needed to be done, I'm already standing in the middle of it and there's no reason for anyone else's shoes to get ruined."

Mayor Harper tilted his head. A beautiful smile bloomed across Mrs. Harper's face.

Snatching the broom out of his hand, she ordered him to take off his shoes before giving him a damp cloth and shooing him into the dining room.

Lexi quickly joined him, but from the tentative way she entered the room, he didn't think she wanted to be there with him.

He could hear the soft murmur of her parents from the kitchen.

Lexi crossed to the antique sideboard—did everyone in town own antiques?—and poured a glass of wine from a bottle sitting there.

She silently offered him a glass, which he accepted. It gave him an excuse to move closer to her.

She poured one for herself and raised the crystal to her lips. Her throat worked as she took a swallow, and Brett couldn't tear his gaze away from the long expanse of it. He wondered how her skin would taste.

"Why did you come into my store?"

Taking a slow sip of his own wine, Brett dragged his gaze up to the deep brown eyes that watched him. "Because I needed a cake."

"Did you know I owned it?"

"No."

Her mouth tightened. She searched his eyes for something, but he had no idea if she found it or not. Either way, she wasn't happy.

"You had no clue who I was when you were flirting with me?"

"I was flirting with you?"

She speared him with a sharp look. Inexplicably, instead of feeling intimidated, he fought the urge to laugh. Not because he thought she was kidding, but because he was enjoying himself.

It had been a long time since he'd verbally sparred with a woman.

But he managed to keep the reaction in check. "No. I had no idea who you were, although I'm not sure it would have mattered if I did. You're beautiful."

She scoffed. The sound surprised him. He was used to dealing with women who knew exactly how enticing they were and had no compunctions about using that knowledge to get whatever they wanted. Which had never bothered him before.

He liked straightforward relationships. He liked things neat and tidy.

He didn't entirely believe Lexi was unaware of the effect her little Suzy Homemaker facade had. He thought it was more likely that her air of self-deprecation was part of the effect.

But it worked.

Brett hadn't planned to touch her, but somehow found himself pulling one of her curls through his fingers. She jerked backward, the heel of her shoe catching on the edge of the area rug. She righted herself before he could catch her.

With disgust, she glared down at the red heels. Muttering under her breath, she flicked her ankles one at a time and flung the shoes into a corner.

With a sigh of relief, she sank her naked toes into the nap of the area rug and her eyes fluttered shut. "Thank God."

Breath caught in his lungs. But before he could do anything, Lexi's parents swept in from the kitchen. They both carried several platters. Brett and Lexi were waved to the table, then everyone settled.

Brett tried to ignore the way his sticky pants clung uncomfortably to his skin. There was nothing else he could do until he got back to the inn. He concentrated on being a good guest, participating in the inconsequential small talk while trying not to let his mind wander to the woman sitting across from him.

Building bridges. Making friends. The first step in his plan to turn the tide in Bowen's favor.

For the most part, Lexi was silent. Her gaze rarely strayed from the plate in front of her. He didn't think it had anything to do with her preoccupation with the meal. She picked at the pot roast, ignored the mashed potatoes altogether and concentrated on a huge pile of roasted squash, carrots, zucchini and eggplant.

They were halfway through the main course before the mayor finally got down to business. "I hate that you wasted your time to come down from Pennsylvania, Brett. The town really isn't interested in the kind of resort y'all want to build."

"But that's exactly why it was necessary for me to come. I'm here to negotiate. To find out what we'd need to do to make the idea palatable for everyone."

"Hiring a new architect would be a good start," Lexi's soft voice finally interjected.

His first instinct was to say something snide, but he realized that wouldn't help so instead he clamped his jaw tight.

"The plans are hideous."

But he couldn't ignore that.

"Hideous? I wasn't aware you were an architect in addition to a baker, Ms. Harper. What eclectic talents for someone so young."

Through the veil of her lashes her eyes punched at him. Flecks of golden brown glittered in the dark depths. But he didn't care. She'd insulted him and his work.

"I don't need to be an architect to recognize whoever designed those plans didn't bother to do any research. We sell quaintly romantic, not Vegas stripper pole."

Her mom nearly choked. "Lexi," she wheezed in warning.

"What?" Lexi inquired, eyes wide with false innocence. "He asked."

Setting his silverware gently on his plate, Brett crossed his arms on the table and leaned toward her. The space between them shrank. She stared at him, no longer lost in the dinner she didn't seem the slightest bit interested in.

The challenge was difficult to miss. He had no idea what had sparked her sudden disdain. No, that wasn't true, it was the same reaction they'd been getting from the moment they'd submitted the plan.

And maybe if he'd been 100 percent happy with that plan he might not have jumped into an automatic defensive posture. But he wasn't happy. Unfortunately, there wasn't much he could do about it. At least, not yet.

The tension between them crackled. Blood chugged thickly through his veins. His voice was low with warning when he said, "I'm the architect on the project, Ms. Harper."

Lexi's eyes widened. "Then perhaps you should go back to the drawing board, Mr. Newcomb, because those plans suck."

Without waiting for his response, Lexi pushed away from the table. "Forgive me for leaving, but I have an early morning." Her pointed gaze found his. "Making chocolate." She rounded the table, pressed a kiss to her dad's cheek and then did the same thing to her mom's.

She stopped to grab the heels she'd abandoned in the corner. As they dangled from her outstretched fingers, she paused in the entrance to the kitchen. "I'm sorry about your shoes."

Brett seriously doubted she actually meant it.

AN HOUR LATER the bottom of his pants brushed stiffly against his calves, rigid with dried sugar and chocolate. The inside of his shoes would never be the same. Hell, even his toes were sticky.

Brett grimaced as he opened the front door to the inn. Getting out of these clothes was all he could think about.

Mrs. McKinnon stuck her head out of the office. "Oh, you're home." Calculating eyes beneath droopy lids swept him from head to toe, missing nothing.

"What happened to you?" she asked, finally abandoning her hidey-hole. Fisted hands landed on her hips and she glared up at him. Brett guessed she was in her late sixties, and as far as he could tell, she ran the place entirely by herself.

He'd never known his grandparents, one set died before he was born and the other hadn't cared that he existed. Mrs. McKinnon didn't quite fit the picture of a grandmother that he'd always had in his head. She was disapproving.

"Nothing."

"That's not nothing." She pointed at his feet. "Those shoes are ruined." She clucked her tongue and transferred the glare from his offending footwear. "You'll be lucky if the pants aren't, too. Take 'em off."

Brett blinked. "Excuse me?"

"Take 'em off." She snapped her fingers and rolled

her finger in the air so he'd hurry up. "I'll have them cleaned and pressed for you in the morning."

It was already well past nine. "They're dry clean only."

"You don't think I can manage to take care of a single pair of pants?"

"No," he protested, not entirely sure why the thought of insulting her bothered him. He didn't know this woman from Adam. Besides, "I'm not taking my pants off in the middle of your foyer, Mrs. McKinnon."

"Oh, for heaven's sake, why ever not? I promise you don't got nothin' I haven't seen." Her mouth twisted and her already wrinkled face creased even more. "'Sides, I don't want you tromping through my nice clean place trailing Lord knows what behind ya."

"The chocolate's dry."

"Chocolate?" she asked, her eyes sharpening. "How'd you get chocolate all over your pants?"

Brett gave up. He'd intended to keep the incident to himself, realizing that exposing Lexi to gossip wasn't the best way to win points with her—or the mayor. But protecting her from embarrassment wasn't worth arguing with Mrs. McKinnon.

"Lexi Harper dumped a bowl of some chocolate thing on my feet."

The wheezing cackle startled Brett. Taking a huge step forward, he started to whack Mrs. McKinnon on the back, afraid she was choking to death, until he realized she was laughing.

Swiping at the corner of her eye she said, "Priceless. They'll get a kick out of that."

"Who will?" Brett asked, not understanding.

Mrs. McKinnon shook her head. "Everyone." She rolled her hand again. "Give 'em over." And waited expectantly.

Brett stood in the middle of the foyer surrounded by furniture that looked as though it might have been in Mrs. McKinnon's family for a couple of generations—small couch, antique lamps, Oriental rug and long sideboard.

He didn't want to take his pants off here. It felt… wrong. So wrong. But she was blocking the only way up to his room and looked as if she planned to stay there all night. He could have picked her up and moved her. Or pushed past her. But she was small and wrinkled, and he just couldn't make himself do it.

Without any other option, Brett kicked off his shoes and reached for his fly. He hopped on one foot to pull off his pants. The memory of Lexi doing the same thing tonight as she'd pulled on her heels surprised him.

With a grimace, he wiped the image from his brain. Folding his pants, he handed them to Mrs. McKinnon and moved to pass her. Her hard voice stopped him. "Socks, too."

With a sigh of defeat, he slipped them off as quickly as possible and dropped them onto the top of the pile in her hands.

"Leave the shoes by the door and I'll see if they can be saved."

"You don't have to—"

She cut him off. "I take care of my guests, Mr. Newcomb, even if they are here to put me out of business."

"I'm not here to do that, Mrs. McKinnon."

Her sharp eyes raked him from head to toe, missing

nothing. Brett fought the urge to cover himself with his hands. The boxer briefs he'd pulled on this morning definitely didn't cover enough. But then, he hadn't intended to be standing in his underwear in front of anyone when he'd gotten dressed today.

Finally, she said, "If you say so," and moved out of his way.

Brett could feel her eyes on his ass the whole way down the hall and up the stairs. Or maybe that was just his twitchy imagination.

It had been a long damn day. Traveling from Philly, meeting with the mayor, dinner at the Harpers'. All he wanted to do was drop into bed and let go of everything for the next few hours.

But he'd barely gotten inside his room before his cell rang. Glancing at the display, he bit back a curse.

"Mr. Bowen."

"How was dinner? Tell me you got what we wanted and you're heading home."

Kicking the door closed behind him, Brett pressed the phone to his ear with one hand while he rummaged in the suitcase he hadn't bothered unpacking yet.

After all the other humiliations of the night, it shouldn't have bothered him to talk to his boss on the phone in his Skivvies, but it did. Peeling them off with one hand, he replaced them with a pair of sweatpants he'd brought to sleep in. Normally he didn't bother, but sleeping on strange sheets gave him the heebie-jeebies.

Not that he was going to tell that to Mrs. McKinnon. Not unless he wanted his pants returned with scorch marks and a hole in the rear. Which, all things considered, was still a possibility.

"No, we did not get what we want."

"What? You had the perfect opportunity to win the mayor over, Newcomb."

"This isn't something that can be done in one night, Mr. Bowen, and you know it. It's going to take repeated conversations and assurances. Compromise."

Something hard crashed on the other end of the line. "Dammit! I need this project to go through, Newcomb. The sooner the better."

"I'm moving as quickly as I can."

The grunt that greeted him sounded full of skepticism. "What next?"

Brett squeezed his eyes shut and rubbed at the headache just starting to invade his temples. He really hadn't thought past tonight. Brett was big on taking one step at a time. You couldn't build the walls before the foundation was down.

"Obviously I need another meeting with the mayor." Although after tonight he wasn't sure the man would agree to see him.

He'd left the Harpers' with the distinct impression that the mayor was smugly laughing at him. They were perfectly polite to his face, nice even, and still he'd walked down the driveway to his rental car wondering where they'd buried the knife and why he couldn't feel the blood seeping out yet.

He'd grown up in a fairly dangerous neighborhood. Guns, drugs, gangs. And these people scared him. Probably because in Philly he knew where the danger lurked. With Sweetheart...he wasn't entirely sure.

Mr. Bowen must have heard the hesitation in his voice. "You don't think that's going to do any good."

"Not really."

A growl rolled through the phone. "Use the daughter."

"What?"

"Use the daughter. I've seen pictures, she's pretty enough. Do what you're good at, Newcomb. Charm her. Get in her panties. Hell, I don't care. Whatever it takes to soften her up. I know those Southern girls. They have their daddies wrapped around their little fingers. If the mayor won't listen to reason then attack him from another front."

Brett sucked in a hard breath.

Lexi Harper was a passionate little spitfire. Her bouncy blond curls, wide mouth and the freckles dotting the bridge of her nose were clever camouflage, designed to draw you in close enough so that she could cut you with her sharp tongue.

One moment she looked like she belonged in the middle of a gaggle of children, and then she became a siren—all voluptuous curves, acerbic wit and blazing eyes. On the outside she looked all soft and cozy, but she'd had no problem putting him in his place. Even now, thinking about the disdainful expression on her face as she'd called his work shoddy, anger bubbled in his veins.

He had the inexplicable urge to prove her wrong.

"I've gathered some information on her—and anyone else I thought might be useful. I'm sending it to you tonight by messenger. You should have it tomorrow."

Brett hesitated. And as always, Mr. Bowen seemed to sense the weakness before he'd even acknowledged it to himself.

"Don't forget that nice little bonus, Newcomb. This is a multimillion dollar project and I stand to make a tidy sum when it finally goes through. If you can get the town to flip I'm not above sharing a cut of those profits with you. Fifty thousand is chump change to me, but it should impress that high-priced girlfriend of yours."

Brett didn't bother telling Mr. Bowen that he and Michelle had broken up months ago. It worked better for him if his boss thought he intended to blow the money on some lavish vacation or diamond ring. If he realized Brett planned to take the money and run...

He needed that bonus. He needed this project to succeed.

"The daughter, Newcomb. Use her."

As much as he hated to admit it, Bowen had a valid point. There was no doubt Lexi had her father's ear. Several times during dinner they'd joked together.

"Look, I don't care how you do it, but convince the mayor to see things our way. Sooner rather than later. You have a week, and for every day after that I'm deducting from that bonus."

Brett's jaw flexed dangerously. He shouldn't be surprised that his boss was changing the rules in the middle of the game. But he needed that money.

"I'll do what I can."

3

"Oh, my flippin' Lord, do you know who's in town?" Hope burst through the back door into Lexi's work kitchen. If it wasn't a normal occurrence she might have jumped. But since the *Sweetheart Sentinel*'s back door was right across the alley, Hope's drive-bys were a regular thing.

Her future sister-in-law was a journalist for the local paper. Well, more than that, really, since her family had owned the *Sentinel* for almost a hundred years. They'd been friends since childhood, so Lexi had been thrilled when Hope finally realized she was in love with Gage.

While keeping an eagle eye on the batch of caramel bubbling away on the range, Lexi reached beneath the counter, pulled out a container of brownies and passed them to Hope.

Her friend sighed with relief and made herself at home, grabbing a bottle of water from the fridge and plopping down into one of the chairs at the tiny table in the corner. She popped the top on the brownies and the tempting scent of chocolate filled the air. Lexi pulled the smell deep into her lungs and held it for several seconds, relishing the only taste she was going to get, before letting it go.

To lessen the temptation, she turned her back and began spreading the caramel in the waxed-paper-lined pan so it could cool and harden before she cut it into squares.

"Do you know who's in town?" Hope asked again, mumbling around a mouthful.

Lexi shrugged. "Maybe, maybe not." How would she know until Hope told her? This might not be the town's busy season, but there were always tourists. Some of them famous. Just last month a young Hollywood starlet had shown up for a wedding dress fitting with Willow.

It was all hush-hush, because she didn't want the paparazzi to get the design early. She'd worn big glasses and floppy hats. Everyone in town had known who she was. But they'd had plenty of practice thwarting nosy journalists when her brother, Gage, a wounded POW rescued in a high-profile military operation, had come home several months ago. The starlet's secrets were safe with Sweetheart.

As were anyone else's, for that matter. There were definite drawbacks to living in a small town, but they knew how to circle the wagons and defend their own when necessary. The mentality was similar to siblings— your big brother could pick on you all he wanted, but the minute someone else tried, blood would be involved.

And anything that affected the town's image, reputation or businesses affected them all.

"Erica talked to Mrs. McKinnon this morning and apparently that prick who's been trying to get the town council to rezone the stretch of land across the lake sent someone for tonight's meeting."

Heat shot through Lexi. Embarrassment, that was all it was. She'd dumped chocolate mousse on his shoes. And told him his work sucked. She'd left her parents' house with self-righteous indignation riding hard, which had lasted right up until her head hit the pillow and she tried to go to sleep.

Then guilt set in. God, she'd dumped chocolate mousse on his shoes and told him his work sucked.

Hope apparently didn't notice her private little meltdown. She snorted. "He came back to the inn last night with his pants in a terrible state. Mrs. McKinnon made him take them off in the middle of the foyer."

"She didn't," Lexi breathed.

Hope's grin widened. "Oh, she did. And was all too quick to pass along every intimate detail she got an eyeful of."

Lexi choked. She wheezed, unsure whether to be mortified on Brett's behalf or amused by the comeuppance Mrs. McKinnon had dished out. Mortification and guilt won. It was her dessert that had put him in the position in the first place.

"Uh…I'm the one who ruined his pants."

"What?" Hope shot forward in her chair. As a reporter, she was used to being the first with any scoop and discovering juicy details after the fact bugged the hell out of her. "How? And why the heck didn't you call me?"

"Dad invited him home for dinner last night. Mama called me for a dessert." Turning to the sink so she could hide her face, Lexi shrugged and mumbled, "I tripped and dumped the dessert on his feet."

"You did what?" Hope breathed.

Lexi screwed her eyes closed, remembering the exact moment the trifle bowl had slipped from her hands. It replayed as if in slow motion. She kept wondering if there was a way she could have saved the bowl—and chocolate. "Nothing."

"Oh, no, you don't." Hope crossed the kitchen, forgotten brownie dangling from her fingers, and pressed her hip against the counter. "What did you dump on his feet?"

"Chocolate trifle."

"You didn't."

Lexi looked at her friend. "I did."

Hope's eyes rounded with horror, but her lips quivered like they were the only things holding back the biggest belly laugh. "On purpose or by accident?"

"Accident."

Hope shook her head.

"But if I'd still had it later, I probably would have done it on purpose."

"That good, huh?"

Lexi grimaced. Giving up on the distraction, she sank into the chair Hope had vacated. The scent of chocolate got stronger.

"He came here and I sold him a cake. I had no idea who he was. He said he didn't know I was the mayor's daughter, but I'm not sure I believe him."

Hope plopped down beside her. "Why?"

Lexi sent her a pointed glance. "Oh, I don't know, maybe because I don't have the best track record when it comes to men who walk into my store. The last one used me for information. The likelihood is this one's doing the same thing."

Several months ago a reporter for the *Atlanta Courier* had targeted her. Brandon had lied, telling her he was a nurse from Charleston, all the while flirting and seducing, subtly pumping her for information about Gage and his experiences in Afghanistan. He'd wanted the scoop on a story Gage had refused to give to anyone—including Hope, the woman he'd loved for years. Luckily, Lexi didn't know any details, but that didn't stop the guilt and self-recrimination.

She should have known Brandon had ulterior motives. Why else would a beautiful and charming guy have been interested in her?

Hope's sharp blue eyes met hers. A single eyebrow rose in a silent question.

"What?"

"Comparing him to Brandon implies that he tried to seduce you. I smell more to this story than you've told me. Spill it."

Fudge. Lexi wrinkled her nose. She should have known Hope would pick up on the one thing she'd meant to keep to herself.

She calculated her chances of getting Hope off the trail and decided they were nil. With a sigh of resignation, she said, "We flirted. Before I knew who he was. But it didn't mean anything and I have no intention of doing it again. I don't trust him."

"You don't trust anyone."

"True."

Lexi eyed the open container of brownies. She really wanted one, but realized the urge had nothing to do with her sweet tooth. Although the nervous pit in her belly would probably feel so much better with a little chocolate.

"Oh, for heaven's sake." Hope reached into the container and held one out to her. "Be bad for once, Lexi."

"No."

Hope rolled her eyes.

"That brownie is a slippery slope. If I break the rules now I'll break 'em again in an hour. And tomorrow. And next week. And before you know it I'll be Piglet Harper all over again."

Hope frowned, but tightened the lid on the brownies anyway. Lexi appreciated her friend's support, even if Hope didn't completely understand. Lexi had worked hard to shed the pounds and the mental weight of being disappointed in her own body. She wasn't about to backslide now because she couldn't say no to a brownie she didn't really need and only wanted because she was embarrassed and upset and on edge.

"So, since you've seen him…"

Lexi ignored the pointed emphasis her friend put on the word *seen*.

"What do you think he's going to do?"

"I'm not entirely sure."

Despite what she'd said about his designs, Brett Newcomb was anything but stupid. She couldn't imagine that he would come all the way to Sweetheart without a plan. And a pretty good one.

She remembered the way he'd watched her with those ice-blue eyes, and a shiver snaked down her spine.

"I've seen that expression on your face before." Hope

watched her with appraising eyes. "You're attracted to him."

"I'm not," Lexi protested, a little too quickly.

Hope's pointed stare weighed on her. It was all her friend needed to call her a liar. It made her want to squirm. And she finally caved.

"All right. So he's…gorgeous. Sexy in a cool, reserved way. If you go for that kind of thing."

"And you do."

"No, I don't."

"Oh, you do."

Lexi reached into the fridge and snatched out a bottle of water, snapping off the lid with one quick twist. "Okay, maybe, if he wasn't the enemy."

"Hardly the enemy. He's just doing his job."

Hope was making excuses for him? She hadn't even met him yet. "Whose side are you on?"

"Yours," was her friend's immediate answer. "Ours. Everyone's. But maybe I'm a little more objective."

"Hope, the man came here to put an eyesore on the outskirts of town."

Hope shrugged. "We both know that's not going to happen. At least not the way things are right now. So maybe he's here for another reason."

Sure, to make her life a tangled mess.

"All I'm saying is you should give him the benefit of the doubt."

Lexi choked on her water and stared at her friend. Had Hope really just said that? Out of everyone, she understood just why Lexi would hesitate to trust anyone, least of all a complete stranger.

Hope had been there when she'd discovered Brandon's deception. "You know what happened the last time I trusted a man who showed up 'randomly' on my doorstep. I'm not inclined to give anyone the benefit of the doubt. Especially a man we know for a fact is here to make trouble."

Hope blinked and shook her head. "What happened with Brandon was not your fault, Lexi."

"Of course it was my fault. I let my lust blind me to what he was really after."

"He was a deceitful user and a talented liar. He'd have told you whatever you wanted to hear."

"Exactly. I should have known it was too good to be true. Guys like Brandon and Brett don't go for girls like me."

Hope's eyebrows buckled and deep frown lines bracketed her mouth. "Intelligent, kind, beautiful and successful women, you mean?"

Lexi sighed. Hope didn't understand. She hadn't lived in the shadows her entire life, crowded out by her powerful father, her perfectly charming mother or her larger-than-life brother. Next to them, Lexi was just… normal. She was good. Not bad, but not stellar.

She was the kind of girl who had to borrow little black dresses and shocking red pumps. Her entire wardrobe consisted of jeans, plain shirts, running shoes and hair bands so her ponytail didn't get chocolate dipped along with the pretzel sticks.

She woke up at five and fell into bed exhausted at nine. And in between she was more likely to have flour and powdered sugar on her face than lipstick and mascara.

And she was okay with that. Lexi had come to terms with who she was a long time ago.

"It doesn't matter. I insulted him and ruined his shoes. And even if I hadn't, I'm not interested. This time there's no chance for confusion. He's only here to get what he wants. Luckily, I have nothing to do with that."

BRETT STARED AT the folder in front of him. A large manila envelope had arrived by messenger this morning. He hadn't had time to worry about it, too preoccupied with preparing for his meeting with the town council, which had been a complete waste of his time.

The room had practically been empty. Only the council and a handful of people had turned out for the agenda. But it didn't matter. Brett had pulled out all the stops, sophisticated presentation complete with fancy graphics, a full scale model and twenty minutes of detailed research for increased town revenue.

One of the council members snored. Halfway through Brett's presentation someone in the audience fell off their chair. The noise got more attention than he did.

Brett was frustrated and not a little pissed.

What had happened to that Southern hospitality they were supposedly famous for? Apparently it was showcased by the spread of finger sandwiches, coffee and cookies. He wondered if they'd come from Lexi, but he hadn't seen her.

And maybe that's what disappointed him the most. After her impassioned outburst at dinner he'd expected her to be in the front row arguing with him. He'd looked forward to the exchange.

Instead, he had to content himself with reading her dossier. He hadn't bothered to grab the others. None of them really interested him. Mr. Bowen obviously had an idea about how this assignment was supposed to go. But he wasn't here. And Brett had his own agenda.

However, the more he spun the idea of using Lexi, the more he thought it might actually work. Partly because she was so completely against the project. If he could convince her of the benefits, her father would have to listen. And if he convinced the mayor, the rest of the council would follow.

He flipped through the pages. Looking at the detailed information Mr. Bowen had provided gave Brett the creeps. He'd included her high school transcript, pictures from her childhood, even how she preferred her coffee. Brett had no idea how the man had gotten the information and probably didn't want to know.

His boss was an asshole, but a powerful one.

She'd been an adorable child, even if her eyes had often been clouded by shyness. She rarely looked at the camera straight on. But her cheeks were rounded with health, and when she didn't know the camera was there the life and light in her expression made his chest ache.

Toward the back, a single photograph caught his attention. Lexi was bundled up in a thick winter coat. It skimmed the middle of her thighs. A hood lined with fur surrounded her face. Behind her, snow-capped mountains jutted into the sky.

It was breathtaking, but not because of the amazing location. It was the smile on her face, the sheer joy and uninhibited exhilaration that caught his attention.

Something told him Lexi rarely let this side of herself free. She was cautious. Methodical. And he could appreciate that since he was usually the same. But there was a passion that ran beneath. Passion he couldn't help but want to see.

Even if he shouldn't.

Now that he knew it was there…

Throwing the dossier into the passenger seat, Brett exited the car. It was late, but after the meeting he'd needed to get away from town before he did something he'd regret. Driving out to the property had seemed like a good idea.

Until he'd realized just how far out it was.

Plop him down in the middle of an urban jungle and he was perfectly fine. But he had no idea what to do with the trees and overwhelming scent of pine.

He was here, though, so he picked his way through the overgrown brush. Everything was lush and green, fully in the throes of summer. A sliver of moon peeked through the branches above him.

He pointed a flashlight onto the unfamiliar ground.

The land was big, fifty-plus acres. For the most part, they were untouched. Somewhere there was a house, but from the pictures he'd seen it was ninety years old and practically condemnable. It hadn't been inhabited for at least twenty years.

The closest Brett had come to this much green space was the park down the street from the apartment building he'd grown up in. And he sure as heck wouldn't have thought to venture out there at night. At least, not without a weapon.

A surprising sense of peace stole through Brett. Bull-frogs called into the night and water lapped gently at the lake's shore. He wanted to see it. From the moment Mr. Bowen had handed him the photographs of this place he'd been drawn to the lake.

He hadn't consciously come here with a purpose, but his feet moved unerringly through the trees toward the water. Stepping out from beneath the shadows, Brett got his first real glimpse. The scent of damp earth filled his lungs. He stopped at the shore, his new shoes crunching on the sandy ground.

Brett stared out across the water to the far shore. It was so…quiet. Here he could imagine the sort of family fun he'd never had. Pushing Hunter's head beneath the water. Wakeboarding. Fishing.

He didn't want to mar the untamed landscape. He wanted to enhance it. To design something that would bring out the character of the place. High ceilings. Walls of glass to bring the outside in. Natural stone. Rough-hewn native woods. Crystal fixtures. Modern rustic.

He could see the building in his head, not that it really mattered.

Even if Bowen would agree, Sweetheart's marketing plan wasn't necessarily geared towards families. But the resort had so much potential to draw in new clientele and increase the exposure they'd already established.

Young parents could bring their families, enjoying a quick taste of small-town life. And after the kids were fast asleep they could take advantage of the romantic atmosphere.

He frowned. Damn Bowen for not seeing the vision. His boss had insisted on a design that was in-your-face instead of integrated with the natural landscape. He'd wanted flashy and eye-catching instead of subtle and sumptuously elegant.

Brett began walking down the shore. His muted footsteps blended with the other sounds—the splash of a fish, the buzz of an annoying insect. The oppressive heat of the day eased and a gentle summer breeze brushed against his skin.

It was difficult to tell where Bowen's property ended and someone else's began. He could see the slanted roofs of several cabins and cottages around the lake. Docks jutted out into the water, some clustered together. Others were spaced farther apart. The lines out here seemed to blur, without many fences.

The beam from his light flashed back and forth across the ground in front of him, more of an afterthought than anything else. He probably wouldn't have noticed even if there was an obstacle in his way. The vista of the lake kept pulling him.

Until the crack of Lexi's voice startled him. "What are you doing out here?"

4

BRETT TURNED SLOWLY. It took several seconds for his eyes to find her since she'd camouflaged herself in the shadows of the trees. Lexi knew the moment he found her, though. She could feel the impact of his gaze as it collided with hers.

Maybe she should have stayed silent, but she'd been surprised to find him out here.

Standing on her back porch, she'd been soaking up a few moments of peace when the bouncing beam of a flashlight in the woods had caught her attention. They didn't often have issues, but this was high rental season, which meant outsiders who were looking for fun sometimes found trouble instead.

She'd grabbed her own flashlight and handgun from the gun safe and headed out to investigate.

The last person she'd expected to see standing at the edge of the lake was Brett Newcomb.

He'd looked so…remote and stunning. Untouchable. And somehow sad. It bothered her. She didn't want to think of him as upset. She wanted to despise him.

Unfortunately, she didn't.

"I could ask the same of you. What are you doing out in the woods in the middle of the night? It can't be safe out here."

His hands popped into the pockets of his pants, pulling the material against his hips and drawing her attention down where it shouldn't be.

"Really?" Her voice dripped with sarcasm. "At least I live out here. I've been running these woods since I was a little girl. You're more likely the one in danger. Do you even know where you are?"

"Bowen's property."

"Wrong. You left that behind somewhere over there." She gestured with her free hand.

The gun hung quietly at her side, but Brett's gaze was drawn to it anyway. His icy eyes sharpened, glittering dangerously through the darkness.

"Why do you have a gun?" His voice was tight with controlled anger.

"I'm a single woman living beside a huge forest on the outskirts of town. We have bears, coyotes and bobcats. Besides, I had no idea who was out here tromping around in the woods after dark. My brother's an ex-ranger. Do you really think he or my daddy would let me live out here without a way to protect myself?"

Instead of mollifying Brett, that knowledge seemed to piss him off. He stalked forward, closing the gap between them.

He crowded into her personal space. Lexi backed up slowly until her spine collided with the trunk of a tree. Brett towered over her, his face dark with an anger she didn't understand.

But she wasn't frightened. Maybe she should have

been, alone in the woods with a strange man who was glaring at her. But she was the one with the gun, even if it was pointed at the ground.

"Put it away," he growled.

Her heart fluttered uncomfortably in her chest. The scent of him overwhelmed the earthy, comforting smell of her woods. It filled her. The wide expanse of his shoulders blocked out her view of everything but him. Heat slowly seeped through her body, radiating from deep inside her belly.

She recognized the sensation, knew exactly what it meant, but didn't do anything to stop it or fan it. Instead, she slowly shook her head. "Not until you tell me why it bothers you."

Lexi had no idea why it mattered, but it did. She wanted to know.

Brett's jaw tightened. He rolled his neck sideways, the cracking sound of it echoing down her spine. But the gesture wasn't a sign of power. It was an unconscious motion while he gathered his thoughts.

"Where I come from nothing good ever happens when guns are around. I spent years trying to protect my little brother and mother from them. I don't like them."

Beneath the heated words, Lexi caught the briefest glimpse of a hunted little boy. He wasn't there long before Brett stuffed him away again, though.

"Please. Put it away."

With slow movements, Lexi lifted the hem of her shirt, took the weapon and popped it into the holster clipped to her waistband. She let the soft material fall back across her thighs, hiding the bulge of the gun.

Brett's shoulders visibly relaxed, easing down. But

he was still close. And without the tension crackling between them, there was nothing to blunt the attraction.

He shifted. The air around her stirred.

Needing something to fill her hands, Lexi reached behind her and pressed them tight against the tree. Rough bark abraded her skin. But it was better than reaching for him and doing something she'd regret.

Brett stood in front of her, silently watching. She didn't like being watched, but his intense scrutiny had the opposite effect from what she was used to. Instead of making her self-conscious and uncomfortable, it made her burn.

A blue flame flickered deep inside his eyes. As she watched, his pupils dilated, pushing against the cool ring of color. Her breath hitched in her chest.

His gaze roamed, snagging on her mouth and pausing so long that her lips parted. She could practically feel the pressure of him there.

Lexi thought he was going to kiss her. Her body wanted him to, but her brain screamed a warning that was hard to listen to.

To her surprise, instead of bridging the gap between them, Brett took a single step backward.

But she didn't want that.

Maybe it was the night. Or the setting. Or the man. But suddenly she wanted to touch him. More than her next breath. And while she'd worked very hard on impulse control in every aspect of her life, tonight those lessons failed her.

Instead of letting him go, Lexi fisted her hands into the front of his shirt and pulled him to her.

On either side of her head his hands pressed tight

against the tree. His tall body angled above her. Beneath her fist his heart hammered against her. That single telltale sign made her want to rub her entire body against his.

He wanted her.

But still he didn't kiss her.

Lexi leaned forward. Her mouth grazed his. It was little more than a gossamer touch, but the low rumble that echoed through Brett's chest had her gasping.

And then he devoured her. With nothing more than his mouth he pulled her in and sent her body up in flames. His tongue stroked deep into her mouth. She sagged against the tree, needing something to hold her up. But it wouldn't be Brett, because he didn't even touch her.

Beside her head, his fingers flexed against the tree. Her own dropped numb and useless to her side. She couldn't concentrate on anything but where they actually touched.

She expected him to be cool and calculating. Instead, his mouth was hot and demanding. She tasted the sharp edge of his desperation and recognized it because she was caught by it, as well.

Need wrapped around her, clenching deep inside.

He sucked at her bottom lip. She leaned into the kiss, nipping back.

Finally, he broke away, ending what she'd started. They stared at each other. His eyes were hooded and hidden. Lexi knew hers were probably round with badly disguised need and surprise.

Never in her life had a single kiss left her so shaken. And needy. Her chest rose and fell with heavy breaths.

The intensity of it scared her. She didn't want this. Especially not with him.

What had she been thinking?

Ducking beneath his arm, Lexi put much-needed space between them. Should she apologize? Probably. But she couldn't find the words.

And he didn't move to stop her. He just watched as she took measured steps. Finally, she turned away, but a few seconds later she heard the rustle of underbrush behind her.

Glancing back, she caught a glimpse of him through the trees.

Was he coming after her? Did he expect to finish what they'd started?

Alarm, seriously delayed and poorly timed, finally clanged through her. She found her voice to ask, "What are you doing?"

His voice was deep and dark, floating to her through the night. "Making sure you get home okay."

Lexi stopped, turning to look at him. Was he serious or was he making fun of her?

His face was half hidden by a tree several feet away. He stood silently and she realized he meant it.

It was probably the last thing she'd expected Brett Newcomb to do, follow her through unfamiliar woods to make sure she got home safely. A startling blast of warmth suffused her chest.

"But who's going to keep *you* safe?"

LEXI WAS A bundle of nerves. It had been one of those days. The kind where nothing went right. She'd scorched a batch of caramel. Her peanut butter fudge seized. It never seized. She hadn't been able to concentrate on anything. Anything except the memory of that kiss.

Why had she done that?

She knew better. She didn't even like the guy. Did she? He had a personal agenda that had nothing to do with the good of Sweetheart. Brett Newcomb had no idea what the town was about. And if he didn't understand, how could he possibly design a resort that would fit?

He couldn't.

What was worse, she didn't think he really wanted to. Those designs—the same ones he'd submitted and presented to the council before—indicated he didn't give a damn.

But that didn't quite mesh with the man she'd found staring across the lake last night. That man had been pensive and quiet. He'd gotten upset at seeing her gun and had followed her back to her cabin, making no move at all to come inside when she'd reached the deck.

Instead, he'd stood in the shadows until she'd closed the door behind her.

The entire town was waiting for him to get frustrated and leave. Lexi wanted him to leave. Or she should have. But the electricity that snapped through her body at the mere memory of his lips on hers called her a hypocrite and a liar.

Needing a break, Lexi popped the "back in 15 minutes" sign onto her front door, turned the lock and headed to the diner to grab something for lunch. Normally she stayed as far away from that kind of fat-laden comfort food as possible—preferring to get her indulgence calories from her own concoctions—but today was an exception. Even she recognized that everyone had to let go once in a while.

But the moment the bell chimed as she walked in the front door she regretted the decision. Brett was there holding court, a group of the old guard spread out across the tables around him. Men who'd been ancient when she was a little girl talked animatedly among themselves.

"He makes a good point," Mr. Luker interjected, slapping the table with his palm for emphasis.

"Maybe, but that doesn't mean we're going to change our minds about the Bowen project," Arthur Edmunds countered.

Lexi wondered if her dad knew Brett was stirring up support. While none of the old guard held any real power anymore, they still had plenty of influence on the people who did.

Brett might not be from a small town, but apparently he knew enough to start with the people who'd been around forever.

With a frown, Lexi crossed to the counter and placed her order. She studiously ignored the group, refusing to turn around and look at them. It might be childish, but it was the best defense she had against him and the itchy need that crackled beneath her skin when Brett was close.

The weight of his stare made her nervous. If he didn't stop staring someone was going to notice. And then she'd never hear the end of it. Just what she needed, to be the butt of even more gossip.

Although maybe it was just her imagination, or

twitchy libido, because the low rumble of his voice continued without missing a beat of the conversation.

Her skin tightened. Her muscles bunched with the need to look, to know whether the scalp-tingling sensation was real or imagined. She fidgeted with the menu, running her fingers up and down the laminated edge. She knew the thing by heart, but it gave her something to do besides wait.

Finally, unable to stop herself, Lexi snuck a quick peek. The muscles in her belly tightened with unwanted anticipation and her mouth went dry. He *was* watching her. But not with the cool stare she'd expected. His light blue eyes burned; heat swept up her skin.

Lexi couldn't look away. Dammit! She didn't like being powerless over her own body. She didn't like the awake, nervous expectation that jangled down all of her nerves.

His mouth moved. Her internal muscles flexed. Without looking away, he continued the conversation. Slowly, his eyelids slipped down, hiding the sleepy, sexy heat from everyone but her. Every cell in her body knew it was there, reacted to the unspoken promise.

"Here's your order, Lexi," Rose Harriman, who'd worked behind the counter for the past ten years, said, finally snapping the connection.

Lexi grabbed the bag, spun on her heel and rushed from the diner, happy to get away from the relentless tractor beam of Brett's gaze. Out on the street she blew a slow, steadying breath. Unfortunately, it didn't quite take the edge away.

She really just wanted to forget that Brett Newcomb

was anywhere close. Easier said than done. Especially since he seemed to be everywhere today.

In between customers and bites of her grilled chicken salad, she couldn't help but notice him crisscrossing back and forth down Main Street. The hardware store. The corner grocery. Petals, the flower shop, although he didn't stay in there long. He even headed into Willow and Macey's wedding boutique at one point. Imagining him in there reminded her of the black dress and red shoes.

When would he leave?

HE WASN'T GETTING anywhere. After a solid eight hours of talking, smiling and arguing with anyone who would listen to him, all he had to show for the effort was a scratchy throat, a pounding headache and a sense that he'd spent all day chiseling at a wall and only managed an invisible chip.

No one in town was interested in being his ally.

If he had any hope of swaying them and getting that bonus, he was going to have to change tactics. If he could get one person to side with him, it would make all the difference.

Lexi, the way she'd looked right after he'd kissed her, popped into his mind.

He headed back to the inn and ended up staring at the copy of the drawings loaded onto his computer. It was either that or the dossier on Lexi, and he really didn't need to read it again. As it was, he practically had the thing memorized.

Starting the design over from scratch was not his intention, but somehow he'd spent an hour with his mouse and CAD program. By the time he looked up it was dark, his stomach was growling and his neck was stiff from hunching over the miniscule desk in his room.

He threw on running clothes, deciding that putting in a few miles would work out the kinks, clear his head, and if he planned it right, he could finish at the diner and grab a greasy cheeseburger as a reward for good behavior.

He never made it. After running the grid of streets around the inn he headed down Main, but only made it halfway. On the opposite side of the street, his gaze was pulled to Sugar & Spice by the magnetic force that seemed to surround Lexi Harper. Asphalt, glass and wood couldn't even blunt it.

His feet slowed and then stopped. Standing in the shadows, he watched her. Her body rocked to an unheard rhythm, her ponytail swaying back and forth. He wondered if the music was in her head or piped through the store.

She pulled out trays, placing them atop the glass case as she transferred her goodies to airtight containers. It was late. He wondered what had kept her tonight.

She paused, swaying back and forth, her eyes closing for a second as she gave in to the music. It was the sexiest thing he'd ever seen. His hands clenched into fists at his side. A half-hard erection tented the running shorts he'd thrown on.

"Use the daughter." Bowen's voice echoed through his brain.

He wanted her. That had nothing to do with the resort and everything to do with Lexi Harper. She was nothing like the women who usually caught his attention. And maybe that's why he couldn't get her out of his head.

The way she'd responded to him last night, he knew she wanted him, too. She might not want to admit it, but there was no denying her reaction.

They were inevitable. Two roads heading toward each other were destined to meet at some point.

He didn't want to sleep with her because he needed her influence. But if that was a perk of having her, he'd take whatever help he could get. This town was killing him and any chance he had at that bonus.

She disappeared behind the red curtain and without realizing what he intended, Brett found himself across the street, opening her door.

5

SHE WAS LATE closing the shop. A last-minute rush order from her online store had taken her almost an hour to prepare, box and schedule for shipment. Luckily, she'd gotten a jump on the baking for tomorrow so at least she'd be able to squeak out an extra half-hour or so of sleep.

Taking some of the leftover inventory into the back, Lexi wished she could juggle the rest of her problems as easily.

The bell at the front door chimed. Lexi cursed her preoccupation. Why hadn't she turned the sign and locked the door? With a sigh, she wiped her hands on the towel hanging from the waistband of her apron and headed to the front. Now that the customer was inside she couldn't order them out. She didn't have much left in the cases so hopefully the sale wouldn't take long.

Halfway through the curtain separating her kitchen from the display area she changed her mind. Brett leaned against the case. Awareness rippled through her belly. He hadn't noticed she was there yet. She could turn around and leave.

His eyes rolled upward, nailing her to the spot. Too late.

She'd just pretend that last night had never happened. He was a customer, like a ton of others she'd helped over the past few years.

"You're smudging my glass." Overcompensating for the unexpected nerves, her voice was harsher than she'd meant.

Instead of being perturbed, a knowing grin tugged at his mouth. It irritated her. She wanted to wipe it away. But not with her own mouth. Not at all. She wasn't going to kiss him again.

"What can I get for you?"

"I was worried about you."

She hummed doubtfully. "You're the one who was hiking strange land in the dark last night." Her body responded to the reminder, flushing with heat. So much for not mentioning it.

His eyes sharpened, and Lexi swallowed. Not good.

"You're usually gone by now."

"Why do you know that?"

"I'm staying at the inn," he answered, like that explained everything.

It was close, but not exactly across the street. Lexi raised a single eyebrow and waited for the rest.

"I notice things."

"Are you watching me?"

His fingers drummed rhythmically against the glass. It annoyed her, not because of the relentless tinkle, but because it drew her attention to his fingers. And made her think about them running over her body.

"No."

They both knew it was a lie. Lexi should be sending

him packing, but instead of finding his scrutiny annoying it thrilled her a little. What was wrong with her?

At least it was nice to know she wasn't the only one losing her head in this situation.

Lexi glanced down at him, for the first time realizing he wore workout clothes. It shouldn't have mattered. So he ran and took care of himself. It meant his body would be hard with well-honed muscles, though. And she wanted to touch all of them.

A pair of shorts hung loosely from his hips and a soft T-shirt clung to a wide chest, molding to his damp skin. Hot and sweaty shouldn't have been appealing. But it was. On him it totally was. She wanted to taste his salty skin.

"Stop looking at me that way."

The low rumble of his words startled her and she jerked her eyes up to his. "What?"

"Don't look at me like that. I did a Google search on your brother last night. The prospect of getting my face bashed in isn't very appealing, and if you keep looking at me that way I'm going to kiss you again."

Lexi sucked in a surprised breath. "What makes you think I want you to?"

His jaw flexed and his eyes sharpened. His gaze snagged on her mouth, and without her consent her lips dropped open, issuing an invitation she had no intention of making.

Triumph flitted across his face. Lexi frowned.

Before she could come up with a proper response he glanced down at the case and asked, "Are these for real?" He pointed to the multi-tiered, gold-rimmed platters of aphrodisiac chocolates.

She'd draped a couple of yards of deep gold satin and lace she'd gotten from Willow's material scraps around the display. Dried red rose petals scattered the surface. Atmosphere. She was excellent at making the product. Thank God she had friends like Willow and Tatum, a talented florist, to help her with the rest. All she had to do every day was replace the chocolates on the platters.

"Yes, they're real chocolate truffles."

"No, I mean are they real aphrodisiacs? Do they work?"

"Yes."

He eyed her askance. "I find that hard to believe."

She shrugged. "Okay."

Lexi had run across plenty of people who thought aphrodisiacs were a bunch of bunk. And then there were the people who swore by them. She fell somewhere in the middle. There was no denying that the herbs she infused her chocolates with had been used for medicinal purposes for centuries. They affected the body. Fact. Whether they affected it strongly enough to prompt people to do and feel things they might not normally, she wasn't sure.

Not that it mattered, really. She'd developed the chocolates as a novelty item a couple of years ago for Valentine's Day. They'd sold so well she'd kept them on the menu. Sure, while she was developing them she'd tested, but not in large quantities. Not for effect, but for taste.

She had no idea if they really worked. Plenty of her customers told her they did and that was good enough for her.

"Okay?"

"Believe what you want."

"You don't stand behind your product?"

"Of course I do. They're delicious."

"I'm sure they are." His sharp, cool eyes cut to hers. "Everything I've tasted has been amazing."

Why did she get the feeling he wasn't talking about the cake he'd bought?

"But do they perform as advertised? I suddenly feel the need for verification."

"Then buy some."

"Oh, I plan on it."

Lexi reached down for a box, ready to start placing an assortment inside.

"But I'm not sure that's enough."

Her hand stilled beneath the glass, halfway to grabbing some chocolates from the top platter. Lexi stared at Brett. His gaze trained on her hand hovering just beneath him as he leaned across the case.

"How will I know if they work?"

Lexi quirked a single eyebrow. "Didn't your mommy tell you about the birds and the bees? You see, when a man and a woman are attracted to each other..."

He laughed, the sound deep and rich as it echoed through her chest. How could his laugh make her skin tingle?

He reached out and tugged at a strand of hair that had fallen from her ponytail. The touch was hardly a caress, but her scalp tightened with anticipation anyway. "Oh, I'm plenty attracted. Would you like me to prove it? Again?"

"No," Lexi croaked out.

"Liar," he whispered, his voice a soft stroke she felt deep in her belly. "You're a hypocrite."

"Excuse me?" She recoiled, only just now realizing how close she'd leaned into him across the case.

"You're a hypocrite, right along with everyone else in this town. What's the loudest criticism for the resort plans?"

"That they're tacky?"

He shook his head. "That they take the theme you've used to build a thriving tourism industry one step too far. Like aphrodisiac chocolates don't do the same thing."

"They do not," she protested, affronted for herself and the entire town. "They aren't tacky. They're sensual and they work."

"Prove it."

They were back to this. "How?" she asked, exasperated.

"Help me test them."

Again she asked, "How?"

"Have dinner with me. Your chocolates can be dessert."

"I don't think so." That was just asking for trouble, something Lexi wasn't in the habit of doing. "Take someone else to dinner."

There was no reason it had to be her. Sweetheart was filled with beautiful single women. Lexi tried to ignore the pinch of spite that hit when she thought of him out with anyone else.

She couldn't have her cake and eat it, too. Either she wanted him for herself or she didn't.

And she didn't.

End of discussion.

"Ah, but there's a flaw in that plan."

If there was she couldn't see it.

"I don't know many people in Sweetheart. If I take out someone I don't know, I won't know for sure if my reaction is from the chocolates or just from natural attraction."

He leaned closer. Lexi wanted to pull back, but couldn't find the strength to actually do it.

"We already know how I react when you're close." His finger slipped softly down the curve of her cheek. She couldn't help it; she tipped her head into the caress, wanting more.

She was in so much trouble.

"You're like a control. If I'm more attracted to you after eating the chocolates—if I can't keep my hands off you—then we know they work."

"You can't seem to keep your hands off me now," she breathed out, the accusation far from as forceful as she'd intended. "Besides, there's a flaw in *your* logic."

He cocked his head to the side and waited.

"I don't need to prove anything."

A grin played around the edges of his mouth.

"True. But you've piqued my interest."

"Your problem, not mine."

"Perhaps, but what if I made it worth your while?"

"How?" She didn't want anything from this man. Really, she didn't.

"What do you want?"

"For you to leave town."

Humor pulsed across his sensual mouth, drawing her attention and scattering her thoughts. What were they arguing about?

"Not going to happen."

Oh, yeah, her chocolates. "Then stop harassing my friends. Leave the business owners alone and find another way to get what you want."

He considered her for several moments. How could his cool blue scrutiny make her insides melt to mush? "Fair enough. If your chocolates work as described then I'll stop harassing your friends."

Lexi's eyes narrowed. She was suspicious. He'd given in a little too quickly, which made her question whether he had any intention of following through on the promise.

"Why would you agree to that?" she wondered aloud.

A wicked gleam crystallized deep in his eyes. "Because I think it's a bunch of bullshit. I don't see how a ball of chocolate can increase sexual desire. It's all up here." He tapped the side of his head.

"What do you get if you're right?"

"A night with you," he said baldly. "I want to kiss you again. It's all I've thought about since you walked away last night."

"Why don't you just ask me to dinner?"

"Would you say yes?"

Slowly, she shook her head. "No," she whispered, not sure if her answer was to his question or his challenge. Or both.

Leaning across the counter, Brett invaded her personal space. He didn't touch her. He didn't have to.

"Coward," he breathed through parted lips. She couldn't pull her gaze away. She wanted to close the space between them and taste him again.

"Are you afraid of me, Lexi? Or of yourself?"

"I'm not afraid of anything."

"Prove it." His words were punctuated with the sensual taunt that dared her to test him—and herself. Did she have the fortitude to tell him no?

Apparently not. "Yes."

Finally, he touched her, running the pad of a single finger across her aching lips.

"You may have the rest of this town snowed with your quiet, efficient businesswoman facade, but you don't fool me."

Lexi pulled back and swallowed, pushing down the lump of nerves that had lodged in her throat the moment she agreed to this madness.

"I've seen the other side of you. Passionate. Fiery. You're strong and determined. Beneath the gingham aprons and cookie dough lurks the heart of a siren. I know. I've seen her."

"You don't know me at all."

"Maybe not, but I want to."

HE'D MANIPULATED HER with that to-die-for smile and his intensely cool eyes. That was all there was to it. If she'd been in her right mind she never would've agreed to have dinner with him.

And to make it worse, she had an entire day to get through before she could get it over with.

After dipping about fifty apples and creating raspberry, lemon chiffon and coconut truffles, she'd jumped on the treadmill and pounded out about six miles. The exertion should have taken the edge off—it usually did. Instead, she was still cranky and now sweaty and in desperate need of a shower.

Luckily, she had a three-piece bath built into the

back. The shower wasn't huge, but it did the job. Although, as she was pulling on her jeans and a pale blue sweater set, Lexi frowned at her reflection in the mirror.

Her face was free of makeup. She hardly ever bothered with it at work. Between the heat of the ovens and her daily exercise routine, it never stayed on long, anyway. Her clean face had never bothered her before. She'd never been one of those women who got excited about experimenting with color on her face.

But today, it bothered her.

She had some time before the store opened. Without second-guessing herself, Lexi headed into the alley that ran behind the row of stores.

Willow and Macey's boutique was four down. She didn't bother knocking, but walked right into the storage room with rolls of fabric, perfectly organized beads and embellishments, and various boxes stacked to the ceiling. On the other side was a tiny office and break room. The largest space was the display area up front and Willow's design studio down the hall.

Neither of her friends or their employees were in the back, which was unusual. Especially since they wouldn't technically open for another forty-five minutes, although, they did sometimes take early appointments.

Walking closer to the front, Lexi heard the soft murmur of voices: Willow's elegant cadence, Macey's no-nonsense, clipped words, and someone male.

Even before she'd walked through the decorative swinging doors that separated the spaces the quickening in her body told her who that voice belonged to. But pushing through and seeing Brett standing at the glass counter, surrounded by tiny beads that caught the light, colored sequins and lace should have made her laugh.

Someone as inherently masculine as Brett Newcomb should have stuck out like a sore thumb. But he didn't. He blended in so easily. The man was a chameleon. She imagined that no matter where he went, he found a way to fit in. Whereas she...she'd always been the one who faded into the background. On the surface those two things sounded similar, but in reality they were totally different.

Blending was good. A skill. Fading just happened. Something she hadn't known how to prevent when she was younger and a comfort zone she was familiar with as an adult.

Lexi's chest tightened. What was he up to now? Whatever he wanted must be attached to the resort. So why weren't her friends slamming the door in his face?

"You could knock down this wall instead, since that one's load bearing. That would actually open up the space, but still give you the clearly defined demarcation that you're looking for."

Willow frowned. Macey nodded slowly. Brett's finger slid across the large square of paper spread across the counter in front of them. It was only one in a thick sheaf.

Stepping closer, Lexi realized they were looking at the blueprints for the store.

Startled by her movement, Willow glanced up. "Oh, Lexi. I didn't realize you'd come in." Her friend smiled. "Everything okay?"

Macey threw her a smile and a quick welcome, but went back to studying the drawing in front of her. "But this assumes we can purchase the space next door. What if we can't?"

Brett shifted. He studied her for several seconds, his face passive and his eyes cool. Then he smiled. And Lexi's stomach flip-flopped.

"What are you doing here?" Her voice was accusing, although she hadn't meant it to be.

Willow's frown deepened and she sent Lexi a cool-it look.

Brett's grin deepened. "You like to ask me that, don't you?"

"Not really, but you're always where you shouldn't be."

"Who knew a public store could be off-limits?"

"Lexi," Willow's soft voice admonished.

Rolling the documents into a tight cylinder, Brett tucked them beneath his arm. "If you don't mind I'll take these with me and have a look at them tonight. I'll see what I can come up with for your existing space."

Macey reached across the counter and laid her hand on his arm. "That would be wonderful. We really appreciate the help. I've been meaning to take the drawings into Charleston, but we've just been too busy. And I have no idea who might be good to talk to."

Brett nodded. "A bad architect can ruin the expansion before it even begins. Let me put out some feelers and see if any of my contacts know someone in Charleston."

The flash of Macey's appreciative smile as she gazed up into Brett's eyes made Lexi see green. Macey was her friend and she was only being polite. But apparently that didn't matter to the green-eyed monster sitting on Lexi's chest.

"You're so sweet."

Grinding her teeth together at the unwanted reaction, Lexi turned away from the group before she said something she'd regret. Brett was in town for a little while. Macey had been her friend—and a good one—for years.

She didn't realize he was behind her until it was too late. The heat of him spread down her spine and across the back of her thighs. All of her internal muscles began to flutter in anticipation. She clamped down on the reaction, but she still wanted him to touch her.

He didn't. Instead, he curled his tall body over hers so that he could see her face. Part of her felt trapped, caught between him and the display rack she'd been pretending interest in. She could have moved if she wanted to, but she didn't. Her muscles were frozen in place.

"I'll see you tonight." His gaze roved over her face, finally settling on her mouth. Her lips pulsed with increased blood and the need for the press of him.

He walked away. Lexi blew out the breath she hadn't realized she was holding. All the tension leaked from her body and she sagged against the arm of the rack in front of her.

Until Willow's voice reminded her she wasn't alone. "What was that about?"

She turned slowly to find both of her friends staring at her with blatant curiosity.

"Uh…"

Macey shook her head, "Oh, no, you don't. Don't even think about pretending that wasn't something huge. I felt like a voyeur and the man didn't even touch you. I've seen plenty of brides and grooms in my day. I recognize sexual chemistry when it scorches up the place. Spill it."

Willow dragged a pretty upholstered chair over. Pushing gently on her shoulders, she forced Lexi to sink. "Jesus, Lexi, you're shaking."

"I'm not." She wasn't, was she?

Willow crouched down in front of her, placing her hands comfortingly over hers. "You are. What's going on?"

Lexi opened her mouth, but she wasn't sure what she wanted to say so she closed it again. Staring into her friend's steady gaze centered her a bit. She found her equilibrium again. What scared her was that she hadn't realized it was gone in the first place. Being around Brett was bad for her health. Or at least her sanity.

"I'm having dinner with him tonight. He called me a hypocrite and challenged me to prove that my aphrodisiac chocolates actually worked."

A telltale grin played across Willow's mouth and she shot a knowing glance back at Macey, who was standing just behind her.

"What?" Lexi asked, puzzled by their silent exchange.

Willow shrugged. "I have to give him points for figuring out which buttons to push. He obviously realized you wouldn't say yes otherwise."

Lexi thought back over their conversation last night. Hadn't he said as much? He'd issued his challenge and then asked her if she'd have said yes to dinner. He'd already known the answer.

"He manipulated me," she breathed, incredulous.

Anger bubbled slowly inside her, starting as a simmer and quickly gaining ground. "He manipulated me."

"That he did," Macey said in that matter-of-fact way she had of cutting straight through crap. "But did you give him another choice?"

"What do you mean?"

"Lexi, you've had a Do Not Disturb sign around your neck for months. Ever since Brandon."

She pushed up from the chair, not wanting to talk about this. But Willow's steady gaze and Macey's raised eyebrow wouldn't let her run from the truth.

"Fine. I've been reluctant to put myself out there again after what happened. And I'm still reluctant. I don't care what Brett wants, I'm not letting him in."

Macey snorted. "Keep telling yourself that."

She wasn't. Although it probably wasn't doing her any good pretending that she didn't want to.

Denying herself was something Lexi was good at. It was a skill she'd been perfecting for years. Brett wasn't chocolate, but she could do the same thing with him. Recognizing and acknowledging her desire to have him was the first step. Reminding herself of all the reasons that sleeping with him was a bad idea should keep her from caving in to temptation.

She'd get through tonight, any way she had to, and then simply refuse to see him after that. No matter how much he baited or cajoled.

And under no circumstances were they having sex.

6

BRETT KNOCKED ON her door. It had taken him a little while to figure out which of the cabins on the lake was hers, but it had been worth the investigation. He hadn't asked her because he didn't trust her not to come up with some reason to call off the whole thing.

And he didn't want that.

His body had been buzzing with anticipation all day. Looking up from those plans at the bridal salon to see her standing there, watching him, had only increased that need.

He wasn't sure what he'd expected when she opened the door to him. He was used to women who spent hours locked inside the bathroom before going anywhere. Women who considered their high heels and skintight dresses weapons in the war of the sexes.

Lexi's feet were bare and her toenails painted the softest shade of pink. Her face had the natural flush of heat instead of artificial crap. Her hair was pulled up into a loose tail, but a few strands had escaped, curling softly against her face.

He wanted to let the rest of it free, to feel the cascade

of it over the backs of his hands as he buried them at her nape and held her close.

Tight jeans molded to her body, but a flowing tunic covered up the good bits that he wanted to see—the curve of her rear and the flex of her thighs. She had runner's legs, her calf muscles tight and perfect.

"Hi," he said, his voice deep and husky with repressed need. Forget dinner, he wanted her. But he had just enough brain cells left to realize hauling her against him the moment the door opened probably wasn't a good idea.

Instead, he held himself in check and offered up the bottle of wine he'd sweet-talked the pub into letting him buy. Thanks to Bowen's report he knew it was her favorite.

"I thought this might go well with dinner."

Instead of smiling at him when she read the label, the corners of her eyes tightened with tension. She didn't take the bottle. Her eyes, filled with wary reluctance, traveled slowly from it to his gaze.

Blowing out an exasperated sigh, he reached for her hand, pressed the bottle against her palm and curled her fingers around the neck. "For heaven's sake, Lexi, it's only wine."

"Yes, but it's my favorite."

"I know."

The wariness sharpened. "How?"

It hadn't escaped his notice that the front door still stood wide open behind him. Was she contemplating shoving him back outside? Too bad. He wasn't going anywhere. Shutting the door, Brett leaned his back against it.

"I have my ways. Are you always this paranoid with your dates?"

"This isn't a date."

He wasn't going to quibble with her over semantics. Not when there were bigger fish to fry. "You didn't answer my question."

"No. Yes. Maybe."

His mouth twisted. "That still isn't much of an answer."

"It's all you're getting."

Someone had hurt her. It was written all over her body. Her shoulders arched close to her ears with tension. Her temptingly wide mouth compressed into an unhappy line. Her eyes kept darting away from him before being pulled back.

She was nervous. Of him. Brett didn't like that. He didn't want her to be nervous. He wanted to touch her, but what he *needed* was for her to relax so they could become friends.

Brett needed her on his side. More than he needed to get laid, although his cock wasn't exactly in agreement with that plan.

Before he'd gotten in the car tonight he'd promised himself he would keep his hands to himself. However, that didn't prevent him from fantasizing about laying hands on whoever had hurt her.

He'd spent his life protecting his mother and little brother from the danger that constantly lurked right outside their front door. It was instinctive. Lexi was so soft and sweet, she pulled at the protective urges that had been lying dormant since Hunter had started college and he'd finally convinced his mom to move into a better neighborhood.

Brett had never felt the need to defend any of the women he dated. They were all perfectly capable of taking care of themselves. Sophisticated, polished, beautiful, competent, none of them had ever needed him for anything aside from momentary distraction.

And that's the way he liked it.

Lexi was perfectly capable of taking care of herself, as well. The difference was that she had a vulnerability that she tried so hard to hide. But he knew it was there.

That instinct alone should have had him walking away. Instead he found himself asking, "Are you going to invite me in or are you planning on serving dinner in the foyer?"

LEXI SLAMMED A drawer closed in her kitchen. It was the best room in her house, where she'd spent the most money. The first thing she'd done when she moved in was tear down as many walls as possible so that she could open up the space. Aside from her store, this kitchen was where she spent the most time, and she liked the open, airy feel of it. She'd offered to cook rather than accepting Brett's invitation to go out because she felt safer on her own turf.

But suddenly, with Brett sitting at the island, a glass of the wine he'd brought untouched in front of him, her roomy kitchen felt too small. She needed more space, but there was none to be had.

So she concentrated on dinner, instead. Cooking had always been her refuge, a way of controlling the food that went into her own mouth.

"Why did you go to culinary school?"

Her eyes cut across to Brett. His fingers slipped up and down the stem of the goblet, but he didn't take a sip. His fingers were strong, capable. She wanted them touching her body the way he was caressing that glass.

To lessen the temptation, she turned away from him and began searing the ahi steaks she'd bought. She already had rosemary-roasted fingerling potatoes and asparagus with hollandaise sauce, but the tuna would only take a few minutes and she hadn't wanted it to dry out.

Shrugging, she finally answered his question because it was safer than letting the charged silence stretch between them. "I've always had a thing for food. In the South we use it for everything. Someone died? Have a casserole. Broke an arm? Here's a cobbler. Celebration? We'll have a barbecue. Good, bad, indifferent, there's always food."

"What's wrong with that?"

She threw a glance over her shoulder trying to figure out if he was making fun of her. It didn't look like it, but with Brett it was hard to tell what he was thinking. His cool eyes and focused gaze were unnerving. She wasn't used to being the center of anyone's attention.

"When I was younger all that food got me in trouble. I had no self-control and was overweight."

"You were an adorable child."

Lexi frowned. "No, I wasn't. And how would you know?"

Something indecipherable flashed across Brett's face, but he buried it in his wineglass before she could figure out what it meant.

"Culinary school taught me how to have the things

I loved, but make them in a way that was better for my body. I found balance." Her preoccupied frown morphed into a smile. "And I'm good at it."

"That you are." Brett tipped his glass toward her in a salute. Taking another sip, he said, "And you're a good judge of wine."

"Comes with the territory. I worked in one of those fancy restaurants in New York for a while. Had to know what paired well with the meal."

"Why'd you come home?"

Lexi plated the food. She glanced over at the dining table and the unlit candles set out across the burgundy table runner. She didn't want candles. That seemed too intimate and datelike.

Sitting at the island was better. Less formal. Surely it proved that she wasn't trying here and didn't care if she impressed him.

She set a plate down in front of him, dropping silverware onto the cloth napkin she'd brought with her. But somewhere along the way she'd miscalculated. There were only two chairs, so she had no choice but to sit next to him.

The warmth from the stove wrapped around her. And the entire meal took on a feeling of careless intimacy. Like they'd been eating dinner together in the kitchen forever.

Maybe some formal distance would have been a good idea.

But it was too late now, so Lexi poured herself a glass of wine. Brett took a forkful of the fish and closed his eyes in bliss. "So much better than the diner food I've been eating."

Lexi laughed. She couldn't help it. "I'd recommend keeping that to yourself unless you want to find your food doctored with Tabasco."

"Why don't you have a restaurant?"

She shrugged. "Chocolate is my passion. Besides, I didn't like the mass-production pressure of an industrial kitchen. I felt…stifled. I like being able to take my time and experiment. Sugar and Spice lets me do that."

Mumbling around another forkful, Brett said, "If you change your mind I know a resort that's going to need a phenomenal executive chef."

Lexi looked down at her plate, her lips twisting. "Awfully sure of yourself, aren't you? Especially after what happened at the council meeting."

"You heard about that?"

She eyed him. "Everyone heard about that. Welcome to small-town life where news travels as fast as the sweet tea can be poured."

Brett shook his head. "How do you stand it?"

"What?"

"The constant pressure and scrutiny."

"I don't. Or I didn't. Why do you think I buried myself in candy when I was younger? As the mayor's daughter I was constantly on display. Luckily Gage's antics took some of the pressure off, but not all of it."

"I'm not sure I could ever get used to it."

Lexi shifted in her chair. "It sounds like your upbringing had its share of drawbacks. Every place has pros and cons. Sure, the ratio of busybodies is fairly high in Sweetheart, but we take care of our own, too. Those same people would do anything for me and my family."

An unexpected lump formed in Lexi's throat. She tried to force it down by taking a sip of wine, but that didn't help. "I'll never forget what this town did for us when Gage was captured in Afghanistan. I'd venture to guess your neighborhood didn't have that kind of support."

Brett's cool gaze shot straight through her. It made her shiver, not because it was distant, but because she was afraid he could see too much. When would she learn to keep her mouth shut? Hadn't Brandon taught her that lesson well enough?

Apparently not.

Jumping up, Lexi took her mostly untouched dinner and scraped it into the garbage. Needing to put space between them, she didn't return to her chair, but reached across the counter to snag her wineglass.

Leaning back against the edge of the stove, she felt more comfortable. Maybe it was the stretch of granite between them or the familiarity of the stove at her back. Either way, Lexi felt safer—not from him but from herself.

Although she had to admit, standing across from him meant that she got to watch as he enjoyed the meal she'd prepared. Lexi liked it when people took pleasure from the things she cooked and created. It was one of the great things about Sugar & Spice. Her favorite customers were the little kids. The ones who shoveled chocolate into their open mouths with abandon until their cheeks were stuffed and there was no more room.

It was happiness. And so was watching Brett eat.

Lexi tried not to preen when he cleaned his plate. "There's more if you'd like."

"No, thanks." His somnolent gaze cut across to hers.

His next words shattered the illusion of calm that she'd drawn around herself like armor.

"I wouldn't want to ruin dessert."

She wanted to think that she'd forgotten just what dessert was supposed to entail, but she hadn't. The relentless thump of blood through her veins wouldn't let her.

Swallowing, Lexi grasped the container of truffles she'd brought home with her. She was reaching for a platter to spread them across when a sound startled her. A Brother Cane song she recognized from her teenage years filled the kitchen.

Impatience cut across Brett's eyes, but he stood up from her counter and walked to the edge of the room anyway. "I'm sorry, I need to take this."

Lexi intended to ignore him—it was rude to eavesdrop—but his exclamation was too loud.

"What the hell happened, Hunter? Is she okay?"

Brett raked a hand through his hair, standing the dark strands on end. She'd never seen him do that before. His hair was always perfectly in place. Was it bad of her to admit she liked it better messy? It made him more…human.

"Okay, what hospital is she in? I'll check flights and get back to you in a few minutes so you can pick me up from the airport."

Whatever was going on couldn't be good if he was ready to hop a plane.

"Sonofabitch, of course I'm coming. No, I do not want you to put her on the—" His voice cut off into a low growl, but quickly changed to a soft rumble. "Mom? Thank God you're okay."

Brett's shoulders drooped. He turned and slumped against Lexi's olive-green kitchen wall. The heel of his palm dug into closed eyes and Lexi realized his skin had gone ghostly pale beneath the normally swarthy complexion.

"I'll catch the first flight to Philly." He paused. "No, I—" and apparently was cut off. And continued to be cut off over and over again. She had no idea what he was protesting, but the woman on the other end of the line wasn't listening. Finally, his head dropped back against the wall in defeat.

"If you're sure. I don't like not being there, Mom. Even if they send you home tonight, you're still going to need a hand for a few days. Yes, Hunter is perfectly capable, but he has school." He grimaced. "Yes, I know I told you this project is important, but not more important than you. If you need me I'll come right home."

Brett shook his head. His eyes popped open, frustration clouding the bright blue depths. She should be embarrassed at being caught unabashedly prying, but she wasn't. There were too many other emotions jumbled up inside her to make room for something as unimportant as that.

Several moments later Brett ended the call, but the whole time he kept her locked squarely in his sights. She could see the barely contained turmoil. The frustration. The fear.

"Everything okay?"

"My mom was in a car accident."

She wanted to cross to him. To offer him comfort.

He'd tried to hide the bleeding edge of concern behind his words, but hadn't quite succeeded. However, she had enough mental capacity to realize staying on her side of the kitchen was wise. But it was tough.

"It sounded like she's going to be okay though."

He nodded, but his mouth tightened. "Some asshole ran a red light and T-boned her. Luckily the passenger side took more of the force. She's banged up, but nothing's broken."

"Thank God."

Brett rolled his lips inward before pushing them back out again in an exaggerated motion that drew her gaze downward. "She won't let me come. Said they were going to release her in a few hours anyway, and it would just be a waste of time."

"That sounds logical."

"But I want to be there. I need to be there."

Picking up his wineglass, Lexi poured him another drink. Grabbing the platter she'd prepared, she brought both with her. "Why don't we sit and talk. It'll distract you."

His hands clenched and unclenched. She could practically see the war going on inside him—go or stay.

His conflicted gaze landed on her. He took the glass she held out to him and downed it in one long gulp. She thought about offering him hers as well, but decided better not.

"You're a good son." Her soft words floated between them.

"Old habits die hard. It's been the three of us since I was nine." His voice was harsh. "There's nothing I can do. I don't know what to do."

Holding out the platter, Lexi said, "Have some chocolate. It always makes everything better."

Brett picked one up between his fingers and popped it into his mouth. And then he took another. And another.

Lexi watched his mouth move and his throat work. She had no idea when the mood around them shifted. One moment she was worried about him and he was restlessly upset. And then the atmosphere changed, and the only thing between them was the snap of heat.

Maybe it wasn't surprising. Brett needed a release and she and her chocolates were easy outlets. He licked a stray smear of chocolate from his fingertips. A tingle crackled down her spine and across the back of her thighs.

She could have pulled away. But she didn't. If she hadn't seen that glimpse of vulnerability she might have had the strength to hold her desire at bay and let him walk out her door.

But she had seen it. And recognized it. That eternal moment of weakness. Instead of pushing him away as she knew she should, Lexi picked out another chocolate and held it up to his lips. His mouth parted. Bright white teeth flashed as he bit into it, slicing it in half. "Mmm, what is this?"

"Chai and cardamom."

"No strawberry or lemon?"

"I have those, too, but the herbs and spices I use have flavors all their own."

She moved to pull her hand away, but Brett stopped her. His fingers wrapped around her wrist, holding her.

His tongue flicked out and ran up the side of her fingers, over the chocolate and back down again.

He pulled the rest of the truffle into his mouth, right along with her thumb and forefinger. He sucked, the pebbled side of his tongue rasping against her. All of her internal muscles clenched tight.

He let her go and she took a step backward. She needed space. Her heart was racing. Her mind was spinning. Her clothes were tight and uncomfortable.

Brett pulled another truffle from the plate and followed her. He held it up to her mouth, but she shook her head.

"I thought chocolate was your weakness."

"It is."

"Then why won't you have one?"

She simply shook her head again. It was too complicated to explain to him. Especially when he was looking at her that way, like he'd prefer to be tasting her.

"Is it the aphrodisiacs?"

"No."

"Then what?"

"I've indulged enough already today."

Brett leaned into her personal space. The scent of him, somehow sharp and decadent, mixed with the spices and chocolate. A heady combination.

His lips brushed softly against her skin. His mouth trailed from her temple, across her cheek and the corner of her lips.

"There's no such thing as indulging enough."

7

WAS IT THE aphrodisiacs or Lexi? And did it matter? Suddenly the idea of keeping his hands off her was impossible. He wanted her. He needed her.

And Brett didn't need anyone.

Wrapping his arm around her back, Brett pulled her close. His mouth crushed hers. She tasted amazing, a temptation that was more devastating than the decadent chocolate could ever be.

Oh. Hell.

Brett had never been this consumed with a woman before. Lexi was different. And he couldn't walk away. Even if he knew he should.

Taking the platter from her hands, he set it on the counter behind her. With deft fingers, he tugged at the elastic holding her hair. It fell, a cool blond cloud that framed her face. He fisted it, wrapping silky strands around his fingers.

Her skin was warm. She made a mewling sound in the back of her throat and pressed tighter into his hold. But she was far from passive.

Her own hands tugged at the buttons on his shirt,

popping them one by one until she found bare skin. Soft palms swept across his chest. Clever fingers tickled over his ribs.

And Brett growled, the sound dark with need.

With his hold at her nape, he angled her back for more. Her fingers ran up the side of his neck and jaw. Wrapping his hands around her hips, Brett swept her up, spinning around. She clung to him, muscular legs wrapped tight around his waist, as her mouth found his throat and sucked.

He was burning and she was the only thing that could quench the fire.

"Tell me where the nearest soft surface is, or in a minute it won't matter," he mumbled between licks and nipping bites.

Lexi arched back in his arms, opening her throat for more. "Who wants soft?"

"Holy hell," he breathed out against her skin. Where was the woman who baked cakes and wore red-checked aprons? The little homemaker was gone, replaced with a siren hell-bent on bringing him to his knees.

"You're an amazing woman, Alexis Harper."

"Trust me, that's the chocolate talking."

He laughed. Her chest rubbed against him, warm and soft. She squirmed. His laughter disintegrated into a groan.

Brett stumbled several steps.

"Put me down, I'm too heavy."

"You aren't heavy, you're perfect."

He could feel Lexi's frown against his skin as she trailed her mouth across his shoulder. Her hands cupped his biceps and her thighs squeezed his waist, hanging on.

Feeling blindly, he yanked a chair away from the dining table. The backs of his knees hit the edge of it and he sank onto the plush surface. She folded around him, her knees bracketing his hips.

Brett let her go, brushing her hair away from her face so he could look at her. She loomed above him, her body arched down as she tried to reclaim his lips. The light from the kitchen fell across her face. Shadows played over the soft curve of her cheekbones and her wide, plump mouth.

Crumpling the table runner in his fist, Brett yanked it until everything on top fell to the floor.

"I liked those candlesticks," she protested. Brett silenced her with another drowning kiss. He couldn't think of anything but her. How she tasted, felt and smelled.

Grasping her waist, Brett lifted her high in the air and set her down on the table in front of him. Her gaze burned golden-brown.

His palms flattened on the polished surface on either side of her hips.

"Stop looking and touch," she panted.

"Are you sure?" He wanted her to be. He didn't want any regrets—for either of them.

"I'm sitting on my table, Brett. It might come as a surprise to hear, but I don't usually do this kind of thing. I'm sure."

He was a blur, he moved so quickly. One hand buried at the nape of her neck as he tilted her backward, the other found the small of her back. He balanced her on the edge, keeping her from falling.

Brett tugged at her shirt, breaking his hold on her only long enough to make it disappear. Her bra was lacy and pushed the curve of her breasts high. His mouth watered. He wanted to pull the tiny peaks deep into his mouth and taste.

His fingers slid beneath the band across her back. She arched against him. His dexterous fingers unsnapped the hooks and the pale yellow straps slid down her shoulders.

Lexi jerked, clutching the material to her chest and holding it in place. It surprised Brett.

Peeling her hand away, he threaded their fingers together. The wisp of satin and lace fell to the ground at his feet, but he didn't watch. He couldn't take his eyes off Lexi.

With a single finger, he trailed across the swell of her breast. "You're beautiful."

She frowned. That wasn't the response he was used to getting from women when he said that. Usually the women he slept with were perfectly aware of their allure. They knew just how to tempt and tease.

Lexi was different and appeared completely oblivious to her effect. Which made her that much more appealing.

With the flat of his palm, he swept against her exposed skin, from nape all the way down to hips. His fingers slid beneath the waistband of her jeans, brushing the top swell of her cheeks. But he didn't go further.

Heavy heat pooled in his belly. The swell of his sex strained uncomfortably against the fly of his pants.

The arch of his nose ran down her throat, across her collarbone and through the valley between her breasts. He breathed deeply, pulling her essence into his body.

"God, you smell good. Sugar cookies. That's what it reminds me of."

Propped on her elbows, she felt there was something wholly erotic about the way he worshipped her body. He trailed open-mouthed kisses and words across her belly, seeming to enjoy the shivers he elicited.

"Vanilla and sugar with a hint of cinnamon."

Lexi shook her head. "Snickerdoodles."

He stilled, twisting so that he could stare up at her from his position between her open thighs.

"Snickerdoodles have cinnamon, not sugar cookies."

Brett cocked his head and studied her. Was she making a joke? "Are you kidding?"

"No, I never joke about cookies."

Grabbing her hips, Brett buried his face in her stomach and laughed. "You are a constant surprise."

Lexi chuckled with him, until the sound was cut short by a startled groan. His teeth nipped at her skin, taking a teasing bite of her.

"I'll take the taste of you over a cookie, any day."

With deft fingers, he made quick work of her jeans. In a few seconds he had her completely naked, a smorgasbord of delight spread out just for him.

It was no accident that he still had every stitch of clothing on. She reached for his shirt, pulled the hem from his waistband and worked it slowly up his ribs. And he let her. Lexi's fingers trailed and played, driving him crazy.

Her hands teased. His fingers found her breasts, rolling the distended peaks of her nipples. She squirmed, making the pressure in his own body build terribly.

Grasping her ankle, he bent her knee and placed her foot flat against the table. With tiny circles, he slowly worked his way up her calf and inner thigh. By the time he got close to what he wanted she was a panting mess, her body strung tight in anticipation of his touch.

Her response to him was thrilling. She was so passionate.

His fingers slid up the crease at the juncture of her thigh. Bending over her, he blew a steady stream of air across her exposed sex. Lexi groaned and her eyes slid closed.

He wanted to sink into her, but one thing was stopping him. "Tell me you have a condom."

Lexi's body stiffened. He knew the answer before she said it, but that didn't lessen the disappointment.

"No. You didn't bring one?"

"Despite what you might think, I did not come over here expecting to have sex tonight."

"You didn't?" Lexi's eyes narrowed.

She was gorgeous, the dark, polished wood of the table the perfect foil for her pale skin tinged with the pink flush of arousal. He wanted her. Enough that it was difficult not to say to hell with the condom. But he wouldn't do that to her.

"Don't get me wrong, I've wanted in your pants from the first moment I laid eyes on you."

"How romantic."

Brett's mouth twisted into a sarcastic grimace. He was usually charming rather than blunt, but he was fighting to keep his sanity at the moment.

"Didn't think you'd say yes."

"Neither did I."

She shifted on the table, trying to pull her thighs together, but his body was in the way.

Frustration clouded her dark-chocolate eyes. "You wanna move?"

Slowly, he shook his head. "Not on your life."

With exasperation, she flopped back onto the table, her arm falling over her eyes and hiding half her face.

"Brett, this is a little embarrassing. I'm naked. On a table. And we're not having sex. I'd like to get dressed."

Her posture pushed her breasts high. They were round, firm and fit perfectly into the palms of his hands.

The flat plane of her stomach rose and fell with each breath. Her body was tense, waiting for him to let her go. But he had no intention of doing that.

Leaning down, he started at the bend in her knee, running his lips up the velvety smooth skin of her inner thigh. She squeaked in surprise, jerking off the table. Her arms dropped away and she stared at him.

"What are you doing?"

"What I want. Do you know how perfectly tempting your body is?"

"No, it isn't."

His mouth found the arch of her hip. He nipped, tasting her. His tongue slipped up over her ribs. She giggled, the sound unexpectedly sexy.

Brett realized Lexi didn't giggle enough. She was so serious and closed off. So determined and focused. She reminded him of himself. But at least he made time to play. Sometimes.

"You should laugh more."

She shook her head, rolling it back and forth against the table. "I laugh plenty."

"Not that I've heard."

"Then tell me a joke."

Brett's mouth curved as it closed around her distended nipple. He sucked, pulling her deep inside. The feel and taste of her was more intoxicating than any wine and more decadent than any food. He rolled his tongue around her pebbled skin, grazing his teeth over the sensitive bud.

"Holy…" she exclaimed. As she arched off the table, her nipple became tighter in his mouth. Her hands found the back of his head and held him against her.

Her body hummed. Brett could practically feel the surge of blood beneath her skin. The same need pounded through him. His slacks were killing him. He wanted to relieve the pressure of the zipper, but didn't trust himself.

With insistent fingers, Brett spread her thighs wide. He trailed kisses down her body, savoring the taste and feel of her against his tongue. His teeth ran over her taut belly muscles.

His fingers found her sex, delving into the slippery folds.

"God, Lexi," he breathed, the need for her throbbing even higher. He wanted to feel the heat of her clenched tightly around him, massaging his aching erection until they both screamed with pleasure.

Instead, he contented himself with gliding a single finger deep inside her. Her strangled hiss might have stopped him if her hips hadn't surged forward for more.

The walls of her sex pulsed around him. Her thighs

fell open wider as she writhed. Brett pulled back so he could watch.

Her eyes popped open, colliding with his gaze. She tried to reach for him, pulling him back down to her, but, prostrate across the table, she didn't have any leverage. He avoided her hands, slipping another finger in and pushing against that sweet spot deep inside her.

Her head rolled backward, lifting everything higher for him.

Hooking his foot around the leg of the chair behind him, he dropped onto the padded surface. He had the perfect view of her beautiful body spread before him. Sweat-slicked skin and contracting muscles. Pink, swollen, drenched sex.

Leaning in, he pulled the heady scent of her arousal deep into his lungs. His own sex throbbed with a relentless rhythm. Running the flat of his tongue up the inside of her thigh, he slipped his fingers out of her.

Lexi whimpered a protest, but sighed with delight when he replaced them with the heat of his mouth.

She tasted unbelievable. Sweet with the bite of something stronger beneath. With the tip of his tongue, he found the tiny button hidden inside and rolled around it. On either side of his head, her thigh muscles flexed and strained.

The harsh sound of her labored breaths echoed around them. His own lungs burned, but he kept up his relentless torture. The need to drive her crazy was stronger than the need to breathe. He wanted her to come apart against his mouth. He wanted to taste the rush of her release and know he was the one who'd driven her to the brink.

Slipping his tongue inside her, he lapped. She quivered and thrashed. She was so close.

As he pushed a finger into the furnace of her sex, she screamed. Her fingers clamped into his hair, holding him right at the center of her body. She tugged, but he didn't care.

Lexi mindlessly rocked against the invasion of his mouth and hand. A few strategic strokes and her body tightened into a bow, on the verge of breaking apart. When she finally let go, the sweet relief of her release wasn't the only thing washing through him.

An intense need. An unbelievable appreciation. Lexi had turned her body over to him completely. That kind of trust was heady and something he'd never experienced with anyone else.

For him, sex was usually nothing more than a biological need. It wasn't beautiful. It wasn't earth-shattering. Those kinds of descriptions had always struck him as fiction.

Lexi made him believe.

She collapsed onto the hard surface, every muscle in her body slack. Her arms and legs sprawled drunkenly and her eyes were screwed closed. Her mouth hung open, sucking in as much breath as possible.

From his position between her open legs, Brett stared up the line of her body. Her hair was wild and in complete disarray, so different from the tight, containing ponytail she always wore. Her skin was flushed, not just from desire, but from the rub of his stubble-roughened cheeks over her body.

She was the most gorgeous thing he'd ever seen.

He wanted her even more now than he had before.

But that wasn't going to happen. Not tonight, at least. Although, if he didn't get out of here in the next few moments he wasn't sure his good intentions would hold up.

The chair creaked when he stood. Reaching behind him, he grabbed the shirt Lexi had dropped onto the cushion. Gently gathering her into his arms, he tugged it on over her shoulders and buttoned it.

Her eyes opened. She watched him with a languid appreciation that did nothing to cool the need pounding through him.

Lifting her up, he set her into the chair he'd just vacated. She smiled up at him, her body melting back against the wood.

Leaning down, he placed a kiss on her mouth. It was quick and chaste, although he didn't want it to be. "Thank you for dinner," he whispered against her skin.

He was halfway to the door when her voice stopped him.

"What are you doing?"

He didn't turn to look at her. If he didn't leave now he was going to lose his head and do something they'd both regret. As it was, his control was about to snap.

"Leaving."

The sultry July air blasted across his naked chest. But he didn't care. Losing his shirt was well worth the gift she'd just given him.

Besides, he desperately needed to cool off.

HE'D LEFT. Brett Newcomb had driven her crazy, given her the best orgasm she could ever remember and just... left. Without expecting anything in return.

She should be grateful to him for thinking clearly when she obviously couldn't. So why was she angry?

All day she'd expected something. For him to call. Or come into the store. Something. But after days of seeing him everywhere, he was nowhere to be found.

Which only pissed her off more.

What kind of man did that and just walked away?

Lexi fought against embarrassment and guilt. She wasn't the kind of woman who expected a man to be her plaything, but this was taking things to the extreme. She did expect to give as good as she got, and Brett hadn't even given her the chance. He'd left while she was still overwhelmed from that orgasm.

Now she owed him. And that didn't sit very well with her.

Although that was assuming he cared to collect.

Part of her worried that he'd left because he hadn't wanted to finish what he started. That the moment he'd seen her naked he decided he was out, but was too much of a gentleman to leave her turned on and wanting.

Lexi groaned. Across the counter Mrs. Voss looked at her like she'd lost her mind. Maybe she had.

Pasting on a smile, she tried to pull her head back where it belonged—to her business. But she couldn't quite stop the telltale blush from flaming up her cheeks.

Lexi worried everyone knew exactly what it meant.

A couple of times she'd contemplated picking up the phone and calling him but decided against it. If he didn't want to see her, then she should be grateful.

Brett Newcomb was totally out of her league. Gorgeous, sexy, charming and worldly. He didn't fit in Sweetheart. No doubt Brett was used to fancy restaurants, museums and everything else Philadelphia could offer that Sweetheart didn't.

The only reason he could have wanted her in the first place was those damn chocolates. She should have known better than to tempt fate and get tangled up in his challenge.

And that was really what it came down to. Even with the boost of aphrodisiac, he'd still walked away.

So it was better this way. She didn't want to see him again.

She didn't.

Although going home wasn't exactly appealing either. It was Saturday and all that waited for her was a lonely night with Little Bits, her skittish cat. She needed a distraction or she was going to drown in her own embarrassment.

If there was one thing she could count on in Sweetheart, it was that on Saturdays the local pub would be full of people watching whatever sport dominated the season. In the summer it was baseball, in the spring, basketball, although nothing compared to the frenzy of college football in the fall. That was just the kind of distraction she needed.

She refused to feel guilty when she locked the door promptly at six and walked out the back. Rarely did she actually leave after closing, but she'd earned a little R & R.

The walk to the pub was nice, the oppressive heat of the day finally easing off. The blast of sound that welcomed her when the door opened was comforting.

Someone hollered her name. Scanning the crowd she realized the place was packed. Gage, Hope, Jenna, one of her good friends and owner of the catering business in town, Aiden, an old school friend of Gage's, and Clay, one of the guys Jenna often hired to bartend, were all crowded around two small tables they'd pushed together. Empty beer bottles and a demolished plate of nachos were scattered across the table.

Hope waved her over. All of the guys were staring up at the screens strategically placed on the walls so every seat in the house had a view of the action.

A groan rippled through the crowd. Clay swore, pushed his chair back and began arguing with the ref on the screen. "He was clearly safe." He looked around for help. Everyone nodded agreement.

"Oh, hey, Lex." Barely taking his eyes off the screen, Aiden grabbed a chair from a neighboring table, squeezed it next to his and waved her into it. His arm dropped casually over the rounded back.

She'd known Aiden for as long as she could remember. He and Gage had played football together. The boy had been a regular fixture at the dinner table growing up. Her mom had often lamented that she didn't have just one growing boy to feed, but an entire plague of locusts.

But she'd secretly loved it.

And Lexi had nursed a secret crush on several of the boys her older brother had brought home, Aiden being one of them. Although she really didn't know why. He was nice enough, but he definitely didn't make her skin crackle.

Not the way Brett did. Her body clenched tight on the rush of need that blasted through her. Damn, all she'd done was think his name and she was in trouble.

Blowing out a breath, Lexi was grateful when the waitress came by and asked what she wanted to drink. Her stomach rumbled loudly, but she declined food. The diner was bad enough. Nothing the pub offered could be labeled healthy. She'd have a beer or two and then head home for dinner.

When a commercial finally broke the tension of the game, Aiden turned his attention to her. "Can't remember the last time you stopped by the pub to watch a game. What's up?"

Lexi shrugged. From across the table Gage's eyes traveled pointedly to where his friend's hand played with the ends of her ponytail. With a sheepish grin, Aiden shrugged and stopped the motion.

The display of big brother aggression bothered her more than Aiden's mindless fingers. Aiden had no real interest in her, and Lexi knew it.

Out of nowhere, the back of her neck began to tingle. At first she thought it was because of Aiden, but she realized the game had come back on and his focus had returned to the screen. His hand was curled around the side of her chair and she'd been completely forgotten.

Slowly, Lexi turned to find the source of the sensation.

And collided with an icy stare.

"Aw, sugar," she breathed.

Hope was the only one who seemed to hear, raising a single questioning eyebrow.

Lexi snapped her head in a quick gesture.

Brett was the last person she'd expected to see at the pub.

8

HE KNEW THE moment she'd walked in the door. His entire body had reacted. The scent of her, sugar and cinnamon, wafted to him on the breeze she let in with her. It overpowered the yeasty smell of beer, sweat and leather.

He'd spent the entire day visiting business owners and had come into the pub to talk to McCallum, the owner, about the potential for adding a pub to the resort, one he could own and run. But it had quickly become clear he wasn't talking to the man today. The place was hopping. He'd stayed because it was the most people he'd seen in one place since he'd arrived. And everyone had been friendly.

Whether it was the beer, good-natured rivalries or just the joy of competition, Brett didn't know. But whatever it was, he wasn't ignoring the opportunity.

Lexi had been on his mind all day. He'd planned to stop by her store later. This morning he'd stopped at the drug store and bought a box of condoms. The clerk behind the counter had stared at his purchase for several seconds before ringing it up.

Brett had never felt so much like a naughty teenager,

not even when he'd been a naughty teenager. He had the distinct impression that everyone in town would soon know that he'd purchased condoms. He wondered if there was a pool going for who he intended to use them with.

And whether Lexi was leading the pack.

Brett's teeth crunched together when a guy he hadn't met waved Lexi over, grabbed her a chair and then draped his arm around her shoulders.

And she didn't seem to mind. Brett waited for her to cast the encroaching arm away, but she didn't. Nor did she fuss at the guy when his fingers started playing with her golden curls.

Anger punched through him. Although he wasn't sure if it was directed at the guy or at Lexi.

It shouldn't have mattered. They didn't have an understanding and she could see whomever she wanted. But not in front of him, dammit. That was taking things too far.

His eyes bored into the back of her skull, daring her to turn around and look at him.

How could she have responded to him so passionately last night and be snuggled up against another guy today?

Lexi shifted in her chair, glancing quickly behind her. Brett knew the moment she realized he was there. Her dark eyes widened and her chest rose on a quick intake of breath.

He couldn't hear the sound, but he remembered the rough rasp of it. A golden burst of desire flickered deep in her eyes before she snapped her head back to the group of people she was with.

That wasn't going to cut it.

Making excuses to the men he'd been sitting with, Brett grasped the slick neck of his bottle and ambled across the room toward Lexi and her friends.

Standing behind her chair, he waited until Gage Harper noticed he was there. "Evening. What can we do for you, Newcomb?"

Lexi's back stiffened and her chair squeaked as she shifted.

"Thought I might join you. Haven't had a chance to introduce myself to everyone."

Gage's expression darkened, but he was too Southern to refuse him. Brett had quickly learned how to use their hospitality to get what he wanted. They were too polite for their own good. Gage offered introductions. When her brother reached her, Lexi cut him off. "Brett and I met at Mama and Daddy's the other night."

The soft tinkle of her voice was a spark to tinder. Spinning a nearby chair around, Brett hemmed her in. She was caught between the asshole who'd had his hand on her and Brett's open knees.

She tried to ignore him, carrying on a conversation with her friends about some new product the soap store was planning on selling. Something about preventing wrinkles, not that Lexi had any to speak of.

For his part, Brett paid attention to the game, interjecting where he could.

And he touched her. His finger flicked up the exposed underside of her arm, right in the crease next to her body. She jerked and nearly spilled her beer.

The guy, Aiden, glanced distractedly away from the game. "You okay?"

Lexi murmured a response.

Brett waited and then he did it again, this time finding the sliver of skin where her shirt had ridden up from the waistband of her jeans.

This time the only reaction he got was a hissed, "Stop that."

Her brother turned hard eyes in his direction. Brett sat perfectly still, staring up at the screen.

She scooted her chair away from his, but thanks to lover boy, could only get another inch or two.

For thirty minutes he kept it up, driving them both crazy. If the fire alarm happened to go off at that moment, Brett wasn't sure he'd be able to get up and run. That's how hard he was. It was a good thing that his position, wedged slightly behind Lexi, managed to hide the evidence from everyone. Although if she'd cared to look it would have been obvious.

But she didn't.

The more she ignored him, the more determined he became to get a reaction out of her, an acknowledgement that something had happened between them. He'd made her come, dammit. With his mouth.

And she'd liked it. He knew she had. Even now, her body quivered wherever he touched. It was the only outward sign that his presence affected her at all.

That and the beer she kept tipping back, downing two bottles in quick succession.

Standing, she spun in front of her chair. Her gaze nailed him, burning brown. "Excuse me." She waved her hands, pushing him back.

He gave her room, wondering if she was going to

run. Instead of heading for the front door, she walked to the dark hallway tucked beside the long bar.

Brett followed her.

BRETT WAS WAITING for her, leaning against the opposite wall, when she emerged from the ladies' room.

He startled her. She'd needed a few minutes away from him, to clear her head. The air freshener that badly masked the scent of bleach had done the trick. For the first time since she'd turned around and found him watching her, Lexi had felt on solid ground.

But there he was, waiting to set her off-kilter all over again.

"What are you doing?"

"Waiting for you."

"Why?"

Without answering her, Brett pushed away from the wall. The kiss came out of nowhere, blindsiding her and leaving her senses whirling.

Her back bounced against the wall and his hands moved over her fiercely.

Lexi had enough brainpower left—just—to pull away. Turning her head, she stared over his shoulder. At least no one could see them, back in the shadows of the hallway. Until a commercial came on and someone else decided they needed to pee.

"What are you doing?" she asked again, only this time her voice was completely breathless.

"Kissing you." His mouth trailed over the line of her jaw and up to her ear. He found the sensitive spot just behind and sucked.

"Why?"

"Because I want to. Because I didn't like watching that guy put his hands on you. Because we have unfinished business." Brett pulled away, staring down at her with sleepy eyes.

Her body responded immediately, melting into a tiny puddle. But the rest of her raised a single eyebrow in challenge. "Do we? What is this, payback?"

Brett's mouth tightened. "Hardly."

"You walk out, I don't hear from you all day, and suddenly you expect me to melt into your arms?"

"Is that what this is about? I didn't call so you're having a snit?"

"Pitching. We pitch snits here in the South. And, no, I don't care if you call me or not."

Cool blue eyes darted around her face, touching her mouth, chin and cheeks before meeting her gaze squarely. He shifted, bringing his body tight against hers, and whispered, "Liar."

And then he was everywhere. Hands and mouth teased. His leg wedged between hers, rubbing against her aching core. She was a liar. She wanted him, possibly more than ever before.

Her hands fisted in his hair, tugging his head back so that she could run her tongue up the side of his neck. He drew a ragged breath through his teeth.

"Do you know how hard it was to walk away from you last night?"

Lexi hadn't realized just how much she needed to hear those words until he'd said them. They were a balm to her wounded soul, healing hurts that he hadn't even caused.

This man wanted her. With the kind of passion that

had him pinning her against a wall in the back hallway of a bar. That knowledge was heady and liberating.

Especially because she wanted him, too.

Tugging at the elastic holding her ponytail, Brett ran his fingers through her hair, scraping it away from her face. "I don't have a lot of control left, Lexi."

His mouth claimed hers again, devouring her with a kiss laden with sensuality and temptation. And Lexi surrendered.

She'd been in McCallum's enough to know where the supply closet was. Fumbling behind her, she found the knob and yanked the door open. She dragged him into the open space with her.

The door clicked shut, closing them together in the darkness. A single tiny rectangular window was the only source of illumination. She could have pulled the light cord that dangled somewhere in the middle of the room, but didn't want to let him go long enough to find it.

It was his turn to ask, "What are you doing?"

"I would have thought that was obvious. I'm seducing you in a broom closet."

Apparently it was all the suggestion he needed. Brett whirled them around. The door reverberated against their combined weight.

Her shirt disappeared over her head. Her bra quickly joined it. His mouth found the bend in her neck where it joined her shoulder. He pulled a heavy breath in and held it. "You always smell so good."

A brittle laugh wheezed out of her laboring lungs.

Tonight, Lexi refused to be the only one naked. The tight T-shirt he'd worn soon joined her clothing on the floor. She reveled in the feel of his chest beneath her palms. For a guy who worked at a computer, his body was remarkably well honed.

The peaks and valleys of his abs were a delight to explore. Lexi wanted to trace them with her tongue, but he wouldn't let her get enough space between them to lean down.

So, instead, she contented herself with running her fingertips down the bulge behind his fly. Brett groaned and a shiver rocked along Lexi's spine.

She tugged at the tab of his zipper, freeing him so that she could finally touch.

Last night she'd been spread out before him, wanting and desperate. Tonight she wanted to make him feel the same way. Needed to know that she could drive him just as mindless.

Shoving his pants and shorts to the floor, Lexi wrapped her hand around him. She wanted to see him, but it was too dark. Instead, she let her fingers explore, learning every hard inch of him.

Up and down, her tight fist slipped over him again and again. His head dropped to the door with a muffled bang as if he didn't have the energy to hold it up anymore. His mouth found her shoulder and he sucked.

His fingers tightened around her hips, digging into her flesh and holding on. "Stop," he breathed. "Stop now."

Brett flexed his hips, pulling his erection from her grip. As he fished in the pocket of his pants, she heard a rustling sound. He held the tiny packet between two fingers, triumph glittering in his darkened eyes.

"Tonight you're prepared?"

"How did you guys survive as teenagers? Thanks to the clerk at the drug store, no doubt the entire town is now wondering who I'm sleeping with."

Lexi groaned, but she'd worry about the implications of that later. Now all she wanted was for him to put that condom to good use.

Her body ached. The emptiness was almost painful. Her jeans chaffed, but Brett made quick work of them. Cradling each ankle, he gently tugged until her legs were free. And the minute she was, she wrapped one leg high over his hip.

His fingers found her throbbing core. He sucked in an appreciative breath. She was hot and wet with wanting him. He played, rubbing against her until she thought she couldn't stand it.

And then the swollen tip of him was nudging her entrance. A little at a time, he slipped inside. And he felt so damn good.

Lexi's body stretched around him, pulsing and begging him to give her more. When he was sheathed to the hilt Brett paused, letting her adjust. But that wasn't what she needed.

Squirming against him, she tried to get him to move his hips. "Please," she begged.

"Shh," he whispered, his eyes glittering at her through the darkness even as his hips gave one quick pulse.

Pleasure spiraled through her. She could feel him so high and deep inside her.

Filling his palms with her ass, Brett boosted her higher. She wrapped her legs around his waist and with the support of the door behind her, hung on for dear life.

Brett drew back and she almost whimpered at the loss of him. But before she could make the sound he was driving back into her. Smooth stroke after smooth stroke, his hips pinned her tight against the door. Which was exactly where she wanted to be.

Her body bowed and tensed. With quick thrusts he brought her to the brink of release and then backed away. Over and over again he drove her straight to the edge but wouldn't let her drop over.

Every muscle was strung so tight she quivered. Fine tremors rocked her body. Her head thrashed back and forth against the door. Her hair was a messy cloud of abandon around her face. She didn't care. The only thing she cared about was what Brett was making her feel.

She whimpered and begged with incoherent words. Hadn't she been the one supposed to make him beg? So much for that plan. She was no match for him.

And then he let her fly. She came apart in his arms, her strangled cry muffled by his own mouth. Wave after wave of bliss washed over her.

Somewhere in the back of her brain she heard his release, her name a guttural groan of ecstasy. Beneath her clinging hands his body arched and strained.

His head fell to her neck. Their mingled breaths joined. She wasn't the only one trembling. Tight against her, his muscles quivered.

Slowly, his mouth trailed across her damp skin. "That was worth waiting for."

Lexi had to agree with him. But now that the blinding need was gone, the unease was there.

They were in the storage room of a public bar.

"Crap, how long have we been gone?"

Through the dark Lexi saw the flash of his frown. "I have no idea. Why?"

"Because someone's going to miss us."

Lexi pushed against his shoulders and dropped to her feet to scramble for her clothes. She pulled them on with more haste than finesse.

"So? Who cares?"

She shoved his own jeans and shirt against his chest.

"I do, Brett. I'd prefer it if the whole town didn't know that we're sleeping together."

His eyes flashed fire before turning ice cold. "But we aren't, are we? So far we haven't gotten anywhere close to a bed. Maybe we should try that next." He turned his back and pulled on his clothes.

Part of her felt relief. Anyone could walk in. The rest of her felt cheated that she could no longer see his amazing body. But now wasn't the time to dwell on that.

"Since you seem so concerned with appearances, why don't you head back out front? I'll wait a few minutes and then follow."

That seemed reasonable. Nodding her head, Lexi reached for the knob, but Brett's hand wrapped around her wrist stopped her.

He pulled her tight against his chest, and traitor that her body was, it began humming all over again.

"Just so we're clear, we're not through yet."

Lexi swallowed. Her heart responded to the dark heat of his words by thumping erratically in her chest. Nodding, she was relieved when he let her go.

She needed space to clear her head. Hurrying to the

table, she scooped up her purse. Hope looked up at her, puzzled. "Where have you been?"

"Bathroom. I'm not feeling well. Gonna head home."

That got her brother's attention. Giving her a hard look, Gage asked, "You okay to drive or do I need to take you?"

Shaking her head vigorously, she said, "No, I'm fine." She fought down the blush that would give her away. Her military-trained brother and her journalist best friend were both too sharp not to notice and wonder what had flustered her.

With one quick glance back at the hallway, she sped to escape before Brett followed her out. Once past the plate-glass windows and any prying eyes, she sagged against the old brick wall.

Good Lord. She'd just had sex in a public place. Before tonight that's not something she'd ever wanted to do. But she'd enjoyed it. Her body shuddered with memory. More than enjoyed it.

What was this man doing to her?

9

BRETT WASN'T USED to walking away from sex feeling slightly disappointed, even a day later. Oh, Lexi had been amazing, but the way she'd skulked away like he was some secret vice she was ashamed of...yeah, he wasn't used to that.

He didn't understand why she cared what anyone else thought.

But today he was determined to find out. Maybe now that they'd gotten some of the heat out of the way he could concentrate when he was around her.

Although, if the explicit dream he'd had last night was any indication, maybe not.

He still wanted her. Desperately. But it was more than sex. He wanted to know *her.* Not just the sound she made when he touched her, but what her childhood had been like and why she felt the need to deny the passionate side she kept buried deep inside.

And he didn't want to learn those things from a dossier.

So, bright and early, Brett found himself standing outside Sugar & Spice. The front door was locked, and the sign said she was closed on Sundays, but her SUV sat in the lot so he knew she was there.

Walking around the building, he found the alley behind and the back door to her place. Unlocked.

Brett shook his head. Turning the knob, he stuck his head inside and hollered softly for her. "Lexi."

But there was no answer.

He walked inside. The scent of something heavenly wafted to him from the ovens. Where was she? She wouldn't leave the ovens unattended. Not intentionally. Brett's heart fluttered uncomfortably in his chest and a sense of dread suffused him. Something wasn't right.

Suddenly a sound caught his attention. He noticed a door nestled between two stainless-steel shelves full of ingredients. Crossing, he tugged it open and nearly swallowed his tongue.

It was a small office. A desk was bumped up against the far wall. An open door showed him a full bath with a tiny glassed-in shower. But what took up most of the space was an industrial-strength treadmill. A yoga mat rolled into a long tube and a medicine ball sat against the far wall.

Brett leaned against the open door, enjoying the view. Lexi hadn't noticed him, probably because the machine was whirring. The treadmill was angled at an incline that mimicked running up the side of a mountain. It faced away from the door, in front of a small TV mounted on the wall. The sound was muted, but one of those do-it-yourself home shows flashed across the screen.

Oh, he'd bet she was good with her hands.

Her feet hit the mechanized track with steady, even

strides. Her skin glowed pink where it was bare beneath the tight exercise shorts and T-backed running tank. A damp line arrowed straight from her nape, down her spine to disappear at the rounded curve of her ass.

He wanted to touch her there. God, he'd never found sweat sexy before, but on Lexi…

Her body was beautiful, the strong muscles bunching and releasing. He could stand there all day and watch her, but eventually she would stop and he'd get caught. Although at the moment, he didn't care if she knew he was staring.

Two nights ago she'd been stretched out before him, a virtual smorgasbord of delight. She was gorgeous then. Last night she'd been so passionate. But now, seeing her body in motion was like watching an artist at work.

He appreciated line and form. Lexi Harper had them in spades.

He waited until her pace slowed a bit. She took a sip from a bottle of water lodged in a holder in front of her. Reaching for a hand towel draped across the bars, she ran it over her face and neck.

Crossing his arms over his chest, he said, "You should really lock the door. Anyone could walk inside."

She yelped and spun around so quickly she nearly fell. The belt beneath her feet kept moving even as she tried to punch the stop button and find solid ground on the runners on either side.

Brett surged forward, trying to steady her. "I'm sorry, I didn't mean to scare you."

Shaking off his hands, she glared at him. "Then what exactly were you trying to do?"

Brett shrugged lazily. He watched her. "I wanted to see you."

"And calling wasn't an option? You had to sneak in the back door and scare the hell out of me?" Her hand pressed tightly between her breasts, as if she were trying to hold her galloping heart inside her chest.

All the gesture did was draw his attention down to her breasts. The tank she was wearing was cut low, revealing the swell of them. The center of his palm tingled with the need to touch her.

But that wasn't why he was here.

Dragging his gaze away, Brett looked into her dark-chocolate eyes and tried to remember why he was here. But it was hard.

And, frankly, so was he.

Obviously, Lexi noticed because her eyes narrowed and her mouth thinned. "If you came for another quickie then you're going to be disappointed."

He stalked forward. Lexi shuffled backward on the treadmill until her back hit the instrument panel. Instead of stopping, Brett followed her up onto the belt. His palms gripped the cool bars, bracketing her. But he didn't touch.

"I didn't come here for a quickie, but we both know if I had neither one of us would be disappointed."

Fumbling behind her, Lexi slapped at the button that would start up the belt. Without even blinking, Brett jumped up, letting the bars take his weight as he planted his feet wide on the runners.

"You're not getting rid of me that easily."

"Why are you here?" Lexi breathed. Her pulse fluttered at her throat, begging him to bend down and taste. Somewhere he found the will to resist.

The sweet scent of her tempted him. It was stronger. Was it her or the store?

"I wanted to see you. Spend the day together. Get to know you."

That wasn't what she'd expected. Her eyes widened with surprise. She shifted nervously on the treadmill and looked away. He didn't understand her reaction.

Brett grasped her by the chin, gently tugged until her gaze met his again. There were golden flecks in her eyes, a warmth that he hadn't noticed before. He liked them.

"Do you want me to leave?"

He watched the war inside her and waited patiently for her to decide. He didn't want to go, but if that's what she wanted....

Licking her lips, Lexi parted them. Without moving anything else, she brought their mouths together. Heat and need blasted through Brett, but he didn't move. Instead, he let her control the kiss.

When he was afraid his restraint was about to snap, Brett pulled away.

She panted, her eyes glowing with a need that he understood all too well.

Shaking his head, Brett took a step away. It would be too easy to give in, but that wasn't why he was there.

Lexi's face blanched and his chest tightened. Dammit! He was out of his depth with her. He had no idea what she wanted or how to give it to her.

"That's not why I came here, Lexi. Believe me, I'd like nothing better than to boost you up onto the bar of this treadmill and take you right now. But I'm not going to do that."

"You're not?" she asked, her voice rough with desire.

"No. I'm going to help you with whatever you had to do today. And you're going to tell me all about your trip to Switzerland and culinary school. I'll tell you about the dog I hid in my room for two weeks before my mom discovered he was there."

She studied him for several moments. "How do you know about my summer in Switzerland?"

Brett swore silently. He tried to control his expression. He'd been staring at that damn dossier too much.

"You told me. I think during dinner at your house."

Lexi's eyebrows crinkled. "I don't remember that."

He shrugged, hoping the motion came off as negligent. "Maybe your mom mentioned it. Someone told me, how else would I know?"

That seemed to satisfy her. She nodded. "No sex?"

"I didn't say that. But the next time I touch you there's going to be a bed very close. And I want to take all night."

Lexi sucked a breath through her teeth. The sound of it echoed through him making all the muscles in his belly clench with yearning. He wanted that now. But he was nothing if not patient.

And he knew it would be worth the wait.

For the next several hours he watched Lexi work. He was surprised at just how time-consuming everything was. She was a perfectionist, testing and tasting until she was satisfied.

At one point she cut her eyes to him as she was pouring crushed herbs into a mixture. "Are you going to admit my aphrodisiacs worked?"

"Why would I do that?"

Lexi's mouth pursed and she shot him a pointed glance.

Setting a hip to the counter beside her, Brett crossed his arms over his chest. It was either that or touch her. And he was trying so hard to be good.

"If I remember right, you were the only one who couldn't keep her clothes on." He leaned closer, filling his lungs with the scent of Lexi and chocolate. "And if memory serves, you didn't have a single chocolate."

Lexi closed her eyes. A shiver quaked through her and Brett bit back a groan. Her grip tightened on the spoon she was using to stir the concoction. The memory of that fist slipping up and down him last night slammed through him.

Swallowing, Brett tried to think about anything but how she'd felt sheathed tight around him.

Her soft voice shocked him. "If either of us had a condom you'd have been naked, too."

Leaning closer, he let his mouth trail just above the curve of her neck. His words caressed her. "True, but that had nothing to do with chocolate and everything to do with the beautiful woman I was sharing dinner with."

"Why do you keep saying that?" She shifted away from him, putting inches between them.

But there was something else.

"What do you mean?"

"Why do you keep saying that I'm beautiful?" She glanced at him through her lashes and Brett was shocked to realize they were a shield.

"Because you are."

"I'm not. You know you don't have to lie to me and tell me pretty things to get into my bed." With a sigh, she turned back to the chocolate she was stirring. "I can't seem to keep my clothes on around you anyway."

That pissed Brett off. Terribly. His hand grasped hers, stopping her relentless rhythm. Slowly, he peeled her fingers from the spoon and set it aside. Gripping her shoulders, he forced her to turn and look at him.

"Nothing I've said to you is a lie, Lexi." Brett's conscience twitched, but he ignored it. Nothing important had been a lie. "You are gorgeous. But I'm not just talking about your body and face, although you have no idea how tempting those are. You're generous and sweet. Passionate and talented. You're the full package."

Lexi jerked her chin from his grasp. Her skin flushed red but he wasn't sure if it was embarrassment or something else. Beneath his hands her shoulders were taut with tension.

She didn't believe him.

"I don't understand why you can't see yourself clearly."

That got her attention. Slowly, her head swiveled so that she was staring at him with big brown eyes. What he saw there made his chest tighten. Wary disillusionment. Sadness. Defeat.

It was so wrong. And so not the passionate and feisty woman he'd begun to know.

She was going to say something, but before he could find out what, a loud knock boomed through the kitchen.

The knob rattled and turned. Lexi took a step away from him and he let her go.

"Jesus, Lex, you shouldn't leave the back door unlocked when you're here alone. No telling who might…"

Gage's voice trailed to nothing. He halted, half in and half out, his hand still gripping the doorknob.

To her credit, Lexi pretended that nothing was amiss. "This isn't Afghanistan, Gage, it's Sweetheart. Nothing ever happens here. Ask Hope, she'll tell you."

Flashing her a pointed glance, Brett had to side with Gage. "You should listen to your brother. Bad things can happen anywhere, even here. Lock your door."

Lexi's gaze bounced from him to Gage and back again. With an exasperated sigh, she threw her hands up and took the spoon he'd placed on the counter to the sink.

"Whatever," she mumbled.

Closing the door behind him, Gage walked into the middle of the kitchen and stopped with heavy arms crossed over his chest. "I distinctly remember breaking a guy's nose in this very kitchen only a few months ago, so I wouldn't say nothing ever happens here."

"Yes—" Lexi threw a dark glance at her brother "—but that had nothing to do with my back door. He was here because I wanted him to be and in fact, if it had been locked you wouldn't have gotten the chance."

Gage's big shoulders lifted and fell. "True."

"What are you doing here?" Lexi asked.

Her brother countered, gesturing at Brett with his chin as if he wasn't standing there listening. "What's he doing here?"

"None of your business," Lexi snapped.

Gage's eyebrows spiked up before slamming down into a dangerous V. He stared hard at Brett, raking him with the kind of expression he'd undoubtedly used to get wayward soldiers under his command into line.

Brett wasn't a soldier, and he'd stared down worse things than Gage Harper's laser-focused gaze.

"What are you doing here?"

Mimicking Gage's posture, Brett crossed his arms over his chest. "Are you sure you want the answer to that question?"

Lexi growled deep in her throat. "Brett, stop tweaking him."

His gaze traveled slowly from the stern expression on her brother's face across to Lexi. She frowned, but a blush covered her skin.

"I just asked a question."

She snorted. "Yeah, right."

Gage surged forward, his fists curled into tight balls that Brett instinctively knew would pack a hell of a punch. But he didn't make it to the target.

Lexi stepped in front of her brother. Slamming her palm against his chest, she stopped Gage in his tracks.

"Move out of the way. I'm going to wipe that satisfied smirk off his face." Gage glared down at his sister.

She surprised them both by responding, "I like his satisfied smirk. I put it there."

Brett nearly choked. God, she was a puzzle. He had a hard time reconciling the woman who'd just refused to meet his gaze when he told her she was beautiful with the woman who stood unblinking between him and a massive guy trained to kill with his bare hands.

She was a tempting dichotomy that he couldn't quite understand. But he wanted to, which surprised him.

Gage's stare blazed with heat, the kind that needed an outlet. Brett had to admit he was glad that outlet wasn't going to be his face.

"Lexi," Gage growled. "Don't you remember what happened last time?"

Lexi's back stiffened and her shoulders straightened. He couldn't see her face, but already he knew her well enough to realize she was glowering.

"Yes, I do, but this is none of your business."

To Brett's surprise, Gage's eyes softened and the wicked glint disappeared. "I just don't want to see you hurt again."

She shook her head, the soft wisp of curls scraping across her back. "Not gonna happen. Not this time."

"That's what you said last time."

Tilting her head to the side, Lexi touched her chin to her shoulder and looked back at Brett through lowered lashes. "This time I mean it."

Brett wasn't sure if that was a warning to him or herself. Either way, the promise made the pit of his stomach tighten, but he wasn't entirely certain why.

He didn't want to hurt her. He wanted to protect her, to give her whatever she needed and to see a happy smile on her face.

Blowing out a slow, measured breath, Lexi looked up into Gage's eyes. "So, other than testing my patience, did you have another reason for stopping by?"

10

GAGE SHOOK HIS head as if trying to pull everything back into focus. "Yeah. Hope asked me to check on you. Need any help hauling stuff to the picnic tomorrow?"

Lexi wished Gage would leave. The past five minutes had been filled with tension and she wanted them over. Had he really needed to walk in right then?

"Nope, got it all covered."

"Hmm," was his only answer. With Gage there was no telling if that was acceptance or a stall tactic while his brain figured out some other way to get what he wanted. "She also mentioned something about a girl's weekend in Charleston that I was supposed to remind you about."

Lexi swore silently under her breath. She'd completely forgotten that was coming up. They'd scheduled the trip weeks ago. A last hurrah before Hope and Gage's wedding in a couple months. Hope didn't want a bachelorette party, so this weekend was as close as they were going to get.

She'd have to remember to call in Annabeth Pierce and see if she could run the store. Lexi really hated to leave her baby in anyone else's hands, especially since weekends were usually her busiest time. But she'd do it. For Hope.

Flashing the widest smile she could manage, she said, "Yep, tell her I can't wait."

Gage flipped one last wary glance at Brett before he leaned down and pecked her on the cheek. "Holler if you change your mind and need a hand."

From behind her, and closer than she'd realized, Brett's voice touched her. "She has two right here if she needs them."

Lexi really wished he'd kept his mouth shut.

Gage trained a knifelike gaze on Brett. Lexi held her breath. She jumped when Brett's hands landed, soft and possessive, on her shoulders.

She wasn't sure that she liked that at all. The testosterone levels in the room were going to kill her. If the two men she was standing between didn't manage to maul each other first.

"Would you two stop? You're like posturing baboons. If either of you starts throwing shit in my kitchen I'm going to be pissed."

Behind her Brett snorted. Gage's lips twitched, but not enough to prevent his frown.

He turned and headed for the back door. "Lock this door, Lexi. I don't want to come in here again and see it open." And with that parting shot, he left.

Lexi sagged, unintentionally letting Brett take the weight of her body. "God, he's a pain in the ass sometimes."

His hands slid down her arms and his chin dug into

the crown of her head. "He's being a good big brother and protecting you."

"His idea of protecting is my idea of smothering."

"Cut him some slack. Having a little brother is bad enough. I worry about Hunter all the time. A sister would have driven me crazy. Especially one as headstrong and independent as you."

"Growing up I was hardly headstrong or independent. I was scared of my shadow."

"All the more reason for him to be protective. Trust me, old habits die hard. Hunter's twenty-two now and I still worry about him."

Brett's hands rubbed up and down her arms, settling on her shoulders. His thumbs dug into the muscles of her neck and the top of her back.

She groaned in appreciation. His hands were magic. And his mouth. And his eyes. And the rest of him wasn't bad, either.

Her brain told her to step away, to put some distance between them, but the languid, liquid warmth spreading through her entire body forbade her to go anywhere.

Lexi realized she didn't know much about this man who'd seen more of her than anyone else in a very long time. At first she hadn't wanted to know. Knowing meant caring, and she couldn't afford that.

She'd had no intention of letting him in. But that hadn't stopped it from happening.

Liking him was inevitable. She wasn't usually the kind of woman who had sex without some connection with her partner. There was no doubt that her body went up in flames when Brett was close. Hell, it went up in flames every time she thought about him.

But that was chemistry and biology. Getting to know him was more.

Soon enough he'd leave for the life he had back in Philadelphia and she'd stay in Sweetheart. Maybe knowing that would be enough to keep her from falling for him. There wasn't a future, there was just right now.

Her body thought right now was just fine. The rest of her was still leery of letting him get too close. It would be so much easier if they could keep this just about sex.

But today had made that impossible. At first, when he'd pulled away from her on the treadmill, his rejection had slammed into her, making her insides ache with it. And then she'd realized he wasn't rejecting her. He wanted something more than a mindless grope in the supply closet.

Happiness and hope had bloomed unchecked. Logically she knew the reaction was seriously stupid, but she couldn't stop it.

"Hunter's seven years younger than I am. While we were growing up our mom worked two jobs to keep us fed and clothed. I took care of him. He's about to graduate with a degree in electrical engineering. I'm hoping he'll be able to come work for me. Eventually."

Pride rang through every one of Brett's words. Lexi tried not to let it matter that he was sharing this with her. Telling her about his family.

"You have the kind of relationship that'll work? The thought of spending every day locked in battle with Gage makes my head hurt."

A shiver of dread snaked down her spine at the mere thought. She loved the guy, but he could be a pain in the ass to deal with sometimes. She had to give Hope credit for knowing just how to handle him.

"Yeah. We get along really well. Don't get me wrong, he pisses me off sometimes, but I'm pretty sure that's normal. We'll figure it out. Besides, I trust him implicitly and would rather work with him than anyone else."

He was close with his family. That surprised Lexi, although she wasn't sure why. Had she expected him to be a smart-ass, driven, results-at-any-cost kind of man who didn't care about anyone and had sprung fully formed from the devil?

Even she realized that wasn't true. And if she admitted it to herself, she had known for a while that he wasn't as terrible a person as she'd wanted him to be.

She wouldn't have been able to sleep with him if he had been. Her libido might not have cared, but the rest of her had some integrity.

The pressure of his hands changed. Instead of soothing his touch became arousing.

"Picnic, huh?"

His stubbled jaw brushed against her exposed skin. Another shiver raced through her, but this one was all electricity and awareness.

"The annual Fourth of July picnic. I'm providing dessert for the entire town."

The corners of his mouth dropped. She could feel the tug at his lips against her skin. "Does that mean you'll be working all night?"

His tongue whispered up the side of her throat. His teeth scraped gently across her thumping vein, making her pulse leap higher and faster.

She'd never been so grateful for preplanning.

"No." Her voice was breathy with barely suppressed longing. "I've been stockpiling stuff all week. And I finished the last of the pies this morning."

"That's what smelled so good when I came in."

Grasping her shoulders, Brett spun her around. The room revolved a little more than it should have. Her head was woozy with single-minded passion.

He stared at her, his piercing blue eyes silky with anticipation.

"About that bed."

THE NEXT MORNING, Lexi bent to load another box into the back of her SUV. She didn't often have to make huge deliveries—like a car full of enough goodies to feed the entire town—but the space was nice. Especially when she catered. Willow had been trying to get her to branch out into wedding cakes, but she'd been resisting. Baking one was no problem, but the decorating…it wasn't her favorite thing and took time away from discovering new goodies to bake.

She'd been toying for a while with the idea of posting at her old culinary school for a baker with those skills. The store was doing well enough that she could afford the expense of more help. And someone who wanted to work in cakes could build that side of her business. Jenna would be thrilled. She often had to order cakes from Charleston or Hilton Head for the events she catered.

Brett exited the back door of Sugar & Spice. He brushed against her, gently pushing her out of the way so he could load in another stack of boxes. While she'd grabbed a couple, he had five balanced perfectly in his arms. His biceps flexed beneath the weight.

"If you drop those I'm gonna be upset."

He flashed her a smile filled with confidence and sexy charm. "I know what I'm doing. These are nothing. I worked construction in college. You should try hauling around cinderblocks and sacks of cement."

Well, that explained the calluses on his hands. And the tight biceps.

She tried to picture Brett with a tool belt around his hips and a hammer in his hand. Of course, after last night, the vision included him without his shirt on. She had to admit she liked the idea of him using his hands.

He was good with them.

But the dress slacks and suits he normally wore were pretty damn incredible, too. They were like pretty packaging hiding the stunning body beneath. Unbuttoning his shirt last night had been like unwrapping a present on Christmas morning.

Lexi's mouth went dry. She wanted to do it again. Right now. But they'd be late, and her mother would never let her forget.

She settled for swiping a tongue across her suddenly dry lips and drinking in the sight of him in tight jeans and a light blue polo that perfectly matched his eyes.

He turned around from grabbing another load and stilled midway to the open hatch. "If you don't stop looking at me that way I really am going to drop these boxes and I won't give a damn."

Heat flared beneath Lexi's skin. "What way?"

"Like I'd taste better than all the chocolate loaded in this car."

Oh, my. He had tasted better than anything she could ever create in her kitchen. It was funny, a few weeks ago, loading all this temptation into the back of her car would have really stretched the limits of her control. All the delectable scents mingling together.

Now the only thing she could smell was Brett, with the underlying hint of sex to tempt her to sin.

"Nothing tastes better than chocolate," she finally said.

The last of the boxes were loaded into the back. Rounding the hood, Lexi jumped into the driver's seat while Brett slipped in beside her.

She still wasn't entirely certain how this had become a joint venture. They'd gone back to her place last night, finally enjoyed her bed and woken up together. Brett hadn't even really said anything about joining her…he just had, pitching in as she'd done last-minute preparations.

The drive down Main to the gazebo and community park in the center of town only took a few minutes. The space was normally used for more formal occasions, serving as a romantic wedding backdrop on most weekends. Today, it was filled with the young and old. At the far end of the open meadow, a bouncy castle and a slide had been erected. A horseshoe pit had been dug and a volleyball net set up. Beneath the gazebo's overhang, the line of chairs normally used during weddings had been replaced by long rows of tables.

A group of men congregated around several large barrel smokers in the gazebo. Her dad and Gage were among them, along with several more members of the town council.

Hope, her mom, Jenna and Tatum, her friend and owner of Petals, the local florist shop, materialized at the back of her car almost before she'd pulled to a complete stop.

Lexi jumped out, using the button on the remote to pop open the hatch.

"I told your brother he should have stopped to help…" Her mom's slightly censorious voice trailed to a startled stop.

Distracted, Lexi looked up from the box that she'd grabbed off the towering stack. Her mom's mouth hung open and her eyes were round. Her friends who'd gathered had the same shocked expression on their faces.

"Good morning." The low, sonorous tone of Brett's voice had a spike of heat and unease twisting through her. Leaning her head around the side of the open SUV, she looked at him standing beside her car. His arm was propped casually against the open door.

He flashed the group of gaping women one of his charming grins. It seemed to galvanize everyone. Suddenly her friends were all busy, chattering and pointing and looking anywhere but at Brett.

Sugar. Lexi crinkled her nose.

Her mom moved forward, offering him a hand. "Nice to see you again, Brett."

He inclined his head. "My pleasure."

Hope snatched her arm, pulling her behind the barrier of the open car. She whispered, "Lexi Harper, what the heck is going on?"

Her other friends joined them. Lexi threw a desperate glance through the window only to realize that her mom had managed to drag Brett several feet away and currently had him engaged in deep conversation.

She probably didn't want to know about what. Lexi just hoped it had nothing to do with her childhood. She'd already humiliated herself plenty in front of Brett Newcomb without dredging up unwanted memories.

"Nothing's going on," she mumbled.

Tatum snorted.

Jenna just stared at her expectantly, waiting for the details to spill. Hope, ever the journalist, couldn't resist the urge to dig.

"Gage told me Brett was at your store yesterday afternoon, but he didn't tell me y'all were sleeping together."

That surprised Lexi. "How do you know we're sleeping together?"

Jenna finally volunteered some information. "Mrs. McKinnon has been telling anyone who'll stand still long enough to listen that Brett didn't come back to the inn last night."

Lexi groaned. Great. In about five minutes the entire town was going to know that she was sleeping with him. Just what she needed. Couldn't she have kept this to herself for a little while? Hell, they'd only just made it to bed last night.

"And even if she hadn't, I'd have known," Tatum offered. "That glow in your eyes and the way he keeps glancing over here waiting for another glimpse of you. Waves of heat are rolling off you both. He'd devour you right here and to hell with what anyone would think."

All of the women around her sighed with satisfaction.

Just what she needed, her best friends spinning this

up into a fairy tale. She was having a hard enough time not doing that herself.

Waking up with Brett beside her had been...amazing. Then he'd made her waffles. And they were good. Carbs weren't her normal weakness, but she could happily gorge herself sick on Brett's waffles.

No man had ever cooked for her. Especially not in her own kitchen. And she hadn't cared.

Lexi was grateful when their tête-à-tête was interrupted by her mother calling for her to hurry up unloading the car. Brett materialized beside her and her friends scattered, carrying boxes of candy, cookies, pies and cakes with them.

"That was interesting," he murmured for her ears only.

"What do you mean?" she asked softly out of the side of her mouth.

"Do you ever get used to the intense scrutiny?"

Lexi's mouth twisted into an unhappy line. "Not really."

Without waiting for his response, Lexi walked away, her arms laden. It took them less time to unload than it did to load because of the extra hands. Once all the boxes were lined up across the tables, Lexi started to arrange the platters she'd brought.

Leaning his delectable rear against the table, Brett watched her. "Why are you doing that?"

"Because it's good business."

"I think your skills speak for themselves. You really don't need the flourishes. Come play horseshoes with me."

Grabbing her hand, he pulled her around the other side of the table. And she let him.

BRETT WRAPPED HIS arms around her, repositioned her hand on the heavy metal and helped her launch it into the air. With a ringing ping the horseshoe connected with the stake.

Lexi whooped. Her enthusiasm launched her into the air. Her hand punched up in triumph. Her hair bounced against his face and her scent clouded around him. With his arms still around her, she slid back down to earth, her back rubbing against his chest.

And he immediately had a hard-on.

He really wanted to spin her around, dip her backward and devour her. Who cared that the entire town was watching.

And they were. The entire day he'd fought the urge to rub a hand down the prickling sensation at the back of his neck. It was disconcerting, being under the microscope. Brett didn't like that.

This town—this woman—made him nervous.

Maybe it was time to put some distance between them.

Lexi spun, her arms ringing his neck, and planted a huge smacking kiss on his cheek. She looked up at him with those sparkling chocolate eyes. Her skin glowed beneath the late afternoon sun.

But not today. And certainly not right now. Not without revealing to the entire town just how much he wanted her.

Apparently, *everyone* was at the park. And while that concept boggled his mind just a little, he'd taken the opportunity to mix and mingle. Lexi had introduced him to plenty of people he hadn't already met and he'd used the chance to talk about the resort. And if he wasn't mistaken, the tone seemed to be shifting. More and more people were actually listening, instead of dismissing him out of hand.

Suddenly, a nasty voice cracked across the easy happiness of the gathering. "Alexis Harper."

Several people around them fell silent. Lexi stiffened, her smile of jubilation fading away to nothing.

Brett didn't like that at all.

A woman—the one he'd seen that first evening in her store—stomped towards them from several feet away.

The old harpy was dressed inappropriately for a picnic. While most everyone around them wore shorts and T-shirts, she'd opted for Sunday best, complete with what had probably once been an Easter bonnet. In full jewelry and makeup, he wasn't sure how she managed not to melt. Possibly through a deal with the devil.

"You should be ashamed of yourself. What a spectacle you're making. Fawning all over this boy. Letting him paw you in public."

Brett couldn't remember the last time anyone had called him a boy. Possibly not since he was ten.

The woman reached out and smacked his arm with the edge of an old paper fan, the kind with a paint stirrer stapled to the end for a stick. The damn thing hurt.

"Where's your pride, for this town if not for yourself? You know he's just using you to get to your daddy."

Lexi sucked in a sharp breath. Her entire body started trembling, although pressed tight against him, he was the only one who'd notice.

Brett's hand flexed around the metal horseshoe still clutched in his hand. His teeth ground together. He was so angry that his jaw wouldn't unclench enough to form the scathing words ringing through his head. Luckily, Lexi didn't have the same problem.

Straightening her shoulders, she turned in his arms to face the other woman, but made a point of keeping his palm pressed flat against her body.

"Mrs. Copeland, I don't believe I asked for your opinion."

The other woman's mouth tightened into a thin line. For the first time Brett noticed that the heavy lipstick she wore had feathered into the fine lines around her mouth, making her look even more like a deranged clown.

"I thought you'd learned your lesson before, but apparently you don't have the sense you were born with."

"My sense is just fine."

"Obviously not. He's handsome and charming."

Normally Brett would have taken those words as a compliment, but the way Mrs. Copeland sneered them sounded more like something a seasoned sailor might say.

"Men like that go for tall blondes with perfect hair, plenty of wit and no stretch marks from an unfortunate childhood."

Around them several people started to murmur. Brett didn't have time to worry about them, he was too busy trying to fight back a blinding rage.

How dare this woman humiliate Lexi this way? In front of everyone.

Ignoring the fact that she'd pegged his normal type

perfectly, Brett growled, "Who the hell do you think you are? You owe Lexi an apology. Right now. She's a beautiful, intelligent and caring woman and any man would be lucky to have her."

Mrs. Copeland wheezed. Her face flushed hotly, but unfortunately, Brett didn't think it was from embarrassment.

"I'd expect you to say that." She smacked his arm again with the flat of her fan. "Men like you always want something and it's never anything good."

Her focus turned back to Lexi. The woman's eyes glowed with indignation and bitter self-righteousness. "Mark my words—he's only using you, Alexis Harper. Everyone here knows it. And when you finally figure that out don't come crying to me."

Lexi muttered, "As if I would."

The heavy heel of Mrs. Copeland's shoe ripped a hole into the grass when she turned and stormed off. In front of him, Lexi's shoulders slumped forward. He didn't like seeing her that way. There was something so wrong about it. She was bright and a fighter. She'd had no problem going toe-to-toe with him any time she'd thought it right.

But Mrs. Copeland's words had taken all the fight out of her.

At least, he thought so. Until he reached out and touched her shoulders.

She jerked straight again, spun on him and blasted him with the burning fire of her anger.

Pushing his hands away, she lashed out. "What were you thinking?"

Brett wasn't sure what he'd expected, but it definitely hadn't been her temper.

"I was defending you."

11

"I DON'T NEED you defending me. I'm perfectly capable of handling her myself. I've been doing it for years."

Through necessity instead of desire, but that didn't really matter.

Brett's eyes flashed hot before going icy cold.

All around them people stared unabashedly. Great. They'd become the entertainment for the afternoon. No doubt the story would be recounted and embellished for the next several hours. And the entire town would weigh in on her relationship. Or lack of one.

She could hear the voices now. Brett couldn't possibly be interested in *her*.

With a sigh, Lexi turned away from Brett, all the fight suddenly draining out of her.

He grabbed her arm, but she shook him off. "Just— just give me a few minutes, all right?" she asked, without looking at him.

Mrs. Copeland had trod all over her deepest, darkest fears. How did the woman always know just what buttons to push to inflict the most painful wound?

But that wasn't Brett's fault. And even as she'd lashed

out at him, Lexi had known that. She needed a few minutes to get her emotions back under control so she could look at everything logically.

Walking back to the gazebo, she found Hope, Willow and Jenna in a cluster by themselves. That's exactly what she needed. Some clear, female perspective.

Walking up, she'd intended to tell them what had happened, but was sidetracked by the snatch of conversation she caught.

"He has a point."

Willow nodded. "A good one. I'm glad I'm not the only one who thinks so." She looked around, her soft eyes studying each of their friends. "I have to admit I was hesitant to say anything though."

"Well, I'm not," Jenna declared, crossing her arms over her chest.

Lexi asked, "What are y'all talking about?"

The three of them exchanged quick glances. Hope shrugged one shoulder. "Brett."

"What about him?" Lexi frowned, not following.

"We've been talking to him and think he has some valid arguments for the resort."

She'd wanted to talk to her friends about him, but this was not the conversation she'd expected to have. "What?"

"Look, he's right. Our businesses all stand to benefit from increased tourism. During the peak season the Briarwood is packed to the rafters. How much business are we missing out on because the inn is full? And what about off-season? I don't know a single business that couldn't use a serious influx of cash during the fall.

Brett has some great ideas on how we could market that season and increase traffic."

Lexi stared at Jenna. With wide eyes, she slowly turned to Willow and then Hope. Her friends nodded their agreement.

"But the plans are hideous," she said softly.

Hope shuddered. "They are, but Brett said they could be changed. In fact, I think maybe he's already got new ones in the works."

That was news to Lexi. And she wasn't sure how she felt about that. She was sleeping with the man and her friends knew more about what he was doing than she did.

It bothered her.

Why hadn't she realized that before now? Was he purposely keeping things from her? Not lying to her, per se, but omitting important details?

This hit a little too close to Brandon. He'd been evasive, every time she'd tried to find out about his life he'd managed to change the subject. Brandon had been slick and cunning.

And while she was intelligent enough to realize it wasn't precisely the same thing, it was close enough that a shiver of dread and remembered pain snaked down her spine.

Was she being stupid? Was Mrs. Copeland right?

Her chest tightened painfully.

"Lexi? What's wrong?" Hope asked, picking up on the distress she was trying desperately to suppress.

She didn't want to give voice to the fears she was struggling with so instead she said, "Mrs. Copeland just had a go at me. In front of everyone."

"Will God strike me down if I pray for her painful and lingering death?" Jenna's falsely sweet voice dripped with venom.

"That woman is a nuisance," Willow agreed.

Lexi definitely couldn't argue with that.

Hope grimaced at her in commiseration. Willow wrapped her in a hug. Jenna offered to slash Mrs. Copeland's tires. All of them coaxed a weak smile from her.

She had no idea what she would do without these women in her life. They always knew the perfect thing to say or do.

Lexi wanted to spill her guts to them. To tell them just how confused she was and completely tied in knots over Brett. Vulnerable. She didn't like to be vulnerable. Hadn't planned on letting herself go there.

The two of them together didn't make any sense.

There was no logical reason Brett should be interested in *her*. Not when there were so many other women around who were skinnier, prettier and more sophisticated. Hell, right beside her were two prime examples. Hope would have been one of them, but since she was already taken...

Mrs. Copeland's words had hurt because they'd rung true in her own head. The problem was, Lexi didn't want them to be.

She was frozen with fear. Holding pieces of herself in check because if she let go completely she just knew Brett was going to hurt her.

How could he not?

She wanted to voice her fears to her friends. They were the most intelligent women she knew and they'd be able to give her an objective opinion.

But the lump in her throat wouldn't let the words pass. And then the moment was gone.

"There you are," Brett said, sauntering up beside them. His hands were stuffed deep in his pockets, but they were jangling something metallic.

He watched her, warily, with those sharp blue eyes that saw way too much. "You okay?"

Lexi nodded. It shouldn't have meant something when he barely glanced at her friends gathered around. But she couldn't help it. It did.

How could he make her feel so…visible? After years in the shadows it was unnerving and exciting and tempting.

She didn't want to respond to him, but her body did anyway. Coming alive, every cell pulsing with anticipation.

Reaching out slowly, he pulled her against him, giving her plenty of opportunity to duck away if she'd wanted to. But the moment his skin touched her own she was a goner.

"You ready to leave? I think I've had about all the Sweetheart fun I can handle for one day." His mouth curled up at the corner in the beginnings of a playful grin.

A few days ago she would have said that "playful" and "Brett" didn't belong in the same thought. But then she'd gotten to know him.

Taking a huge breath, Lexi held it inside her body, letting all of her cells absorb the clean, crisp scent of him. It calmed her. Took away the sting of the past half hour.

But it couldn't quite wipe away the niggling sensation of impending doom.

This was too good, and in Lexi's experience that meant something terrible was going to happen.

It always did.

THE DRIVE BACK to Lexi's was quiet. The heavier the silence between them got, the more his body tightened. He kept pulling glances at her, trying to gauge what she was thinking. Not that her calm, still face gave anything away.

He sucked at this.

He wasn't good at it. Emotion and relationships baffled him and always had. This was precisely why he preferred women who didn't give a damn about anything but themselves. It was so much easier. At least then he always knew where he stood and what reaction to expect.

But that so wasn't Lexi. She was sweet and giving and he could tell that the harpy's attack had really hurt her. She was upset, and it bothered him because she wasn't talking to him. Worse, he had no idea how to fix it.

Even realizing he wanted to was a revelation. One he didn't have a clue what to do with.

Following her inside, he watched as she dropped her purse and bag on the small table in the front hall.

A ball of fur streaked from the back of the house to curl around her ankles. Lexi bent down, rubbed her hand back and forth across the cat's arching back.

"Who's that?" Brett asked. He'd only taken a few steps inside. Unlike before when her house had felt so inviting and warm, he couldn't shake the sensation that she didn't want him there.

She was pulling back and he had no idea how to stop her.

"Little Bits," she answered, glancing up at him through lowered lashes.

"Is she new?"

Lexi shook her head and went back to rubbing the soft, fluffy fur. She was a mottled mixture of black, tan and white with a stripe perfectly bisecting her face. "She doesn't usually come out when strangers are around."

The cat stopped between Lexi's open feet, sheltered beneath her crouched body and speared him with shrewd green eyes.

Her owner watched him as well, with that same wary expression she'd worn when they first met.

He didn't like it. That expression made his stomach churn. To counter the sensation, he crouched down, hands pressed against bent knees.

"Skittish. Like her owner." Brett held his palm out flat. He wasn't sure whether he was reaching out to Lexi or Little Bits.

Lexi stayed where she was, but despite carrying a few extra pounds, the cat daintily picked her way across the space between them and pushed her head against his outstretched hand. Brett let her take the lead. After a few moments she was weaving between his legs.

He'd never had a pet. When he was growing up, it would have just been one more mouth to feed, and they had enough trouble with the humans in the house. In college he hadn't had the time. Now, he hadn't thought he was the kind of person who needed another soul around to be content.

But he had to admit it was kind of nice. A soft sense of peace settled over him.

Unfortunately, it was easily shattered.

Standing, Lexi startled Little Bits, who bolted for the back of the house and whatever hidey-hole she preferred.

Lexi crossed her arms over her chest and stared down at him. Her expression was passive, but her eyes roiled with turmoil. Brett waited, his empty hands dangling between open knees as he enjoyed the view of her small, curvy body from his perfect vantage point.

"I think you should go."

Pushing to his feet, he didn't like the way she took a single step away from him. She'd become as edgy as the cat.

"Why?"

She swallowed and shook her head. That wasn't going to work for him. If she wanted to give him the brush-off he wasn't going to make it easy for her. She was going to have to tell him why. What had he done?

He took another step closer. She moved back again. Brett continued to push until her shoulders collided with the wall. He towered above her and for the first time since he'd met her he realized just how small she really was.

It was easy to forget. Like a porcupine with quills constantly at the ready, Lexi seemed to always be on the offensive. She appeared so strong and secure on the outside.

He was just now starting to realize how much of a

facade it really was. Patched together, the cracks were beginning to show. But rather than making her less appealing, they made her more. He wanted to be the one to shore up her vulnerabilities.

The idea of her hurting bothered him. A lot.

"What's going on, Lexi?"

Even now, she tried to brazen it out, straightening her shoulders and pulling every spare centimeter out of her full height. "Nothing's going on, Brett. It's been a long few days. I'm tired. I'd like to be alone."

Brett watched her lips as she spoke. Her soft, wide and beautifully imperfect mouth. He wanted to kiss her. To taste her. To overwhelm her so she'd forget whatever was going on. But he didn't think that was a smart idea. At least not yet.

Studiously, he pulled his gaze away so that he could look into her eyes. And there he found the truth. The tiny spark of hurt that she couldn't completely hide.

Her ponytail had fallen across her shoulder, trailing down to the edge of her collarbone and lying against the soft cotton of her shirt. He reached for the riotous curls and tried not to care when she flinched away from his touch.

"What was Mrs. Copeland talking about?"

Lexi dipped her head sideways, tugging her hair away from his fingers. "Nothing."

Bending down, Brett pressed his nose against the curve of her neck. He breathed deeply, pulling that cinnamon and sugar scent deep into his body. The pulse at the base of her throat leapt.

"Liar."

For several seconds Brett lost the train of his intent.

Caught in the spell that her body was weaving around him, all he wanted was to close the space between them and feel—her, him, everything.

Somewhere in the back of his brain he found the strength to pull away from her. This was important.

His hands bracketed her throat. His fingers wove into the hair at her nape and his thumbs brushed down the smooth curve of her skin. Angling her head, he gently forced her to look him in the eye.

And just like the skittish cat, he held her for several seconds and waited. He watched the play of emotion through her eyes. The rest of her face remained perfectly passive. He hated that she'd perfected that blank canvas. He wanted to hurt everything and everyone who'd had a part in teaching her the need for self-preservation.

But that was another conversation for another time.

Instead, he focused on the internal struggle she couldn't quite keep hidden. Animosity, fear, alienation, envy, hope and eventually resignation all filled her.

With a twist of her lips, she said, "You aren't going to leave until I tell you, are you?"

Slowly, he shook his head.

Blowing out an unhappy breath, she said, "Fine. A few months ago I started dating a guy who used me to get to my brother. He was a reporter and wanted a story. I stupidly gave it to him."

Brett let her words settle. He ran them through and matched them against everything he'd learned about her. And wondered how Bowen had missed that little tidbit. Surely he would have included any news articles that involved her name.

The disgust she felt—for both the reporter and herself—was evident. The way she'd spit out the story was telling enough. But there was more beneath.

"You trusted him."

"Of course I trusted him." She jerked against his hold, trying to break eye contact, but he wouldn't let her go.

"You don't trust easily."

It wasn't a question, it was a statement. He'd already figured that out about her. From the first moment they met she'd been hesitant. Maybe now she'd tell him why.

"Not anymore. If the only reason people cared about you was because of who your father was? Or your brother? Or the only friends you had growing up were the daughters of your mother's friends because they weren't given a choice?"

Probably not. If everyone around him had had ulterior motives for being pleasant it would be natural to question everyone and everything. And so much easier just not to bother.

The picture she painted of her childhood made him sad. There was a vulnerability lurking beneath the "stay away" signal she couldn't quite keep turned on.

He'd had things rough, but at the end of the day his mother and brother loved and supported him. They'd tackled any challenges together and he would always be grateful for that.

But he'd met her parents and they were perfectly nice people. He couldn't imagine them sitting idly by while Lexi hurt. Or her brother, for that matter. Even now as an adult, he was overprotective. But maybe that tendency had started after his time at war.

Either way, Brett wished he'd been there to protect her the same way he'd protected Hunter from all the bullies and gangs who'd wanted to sink their claws into him.

But he didn't think giving Lexi his sympathy would get him anywhere. Especially right now. She was proud and stronger than she gave herself credit for. Sympathy was the last thing she'd want. Even if she had it.

"You don't trust me."

"I don't know you."

That was so wrong. For the first time Brett realized that he'd shown her pieces of his life he hadn't shared with anyone. He'd told her about his brother and mother. Hell, his last girlfriend had thought he was an orphan. And he'd liked it that way so he hadn't disabused her of the assumption. He'd had no intention of introducing her to his family. Or vice versa.

His mom would love Lexi. So would Hunter. He could see the two of them teasing each other, his sharp-tongued brother and sweet Lexi.

Before he could stop the confession, Brett found himself admitting, "You know me better than you think."

She scoffed at his words.

Brett tightened his hold on her nape, bent his knees and brought Lexi close. He stared into her eyes, hoping she could see the truth. "I don't care who your dad is. Or your brother or your mother. I don't care what the rest of the town thinks, and you shouldn't either."

"Easy for you to say. You'll leave in a few weeks and I'll still have to deal with them."

Her words sent a ribbon of unease slithering through

him. He pushed the reaction aside, not wanting to examine it too closely.

"Me being here, right now, with you, has nothing to do with the resort, Lexi. I promise you that."

Her mouth tightened and her eyes brightened. "Are you asking me to trust you?"

"I'm telling you that you can."

"What's the difference?"

"This," he breathed, closing the space between them and claiming her mouth.

12

THE KISS STARTED off soft, persuasive. But it quickly turned hot and sticky, like the best hot fudge. The passion that flared between them was hard for Lexi to deny. She'd never been this overwhelmed by anyone, certainly not Brandon.

Brett was nothing like Brandon, the man she'd been attracted to months ago. Looking back, it had been easy to spot the slick lies and half-truths he'd told. His ill-disguised wheedling practically had blinking warning lights.

Which is what scared her the most. At the time, Lexi had been completely oblivious. What if she was blinded again? Blinded by need, a sexy man and feelings she wasn't quite ready to acknowledge?

He broke away from her. They both panted and Lexi's mind whirled. What to do?

Send him away or trust? Her brain clamored for her to protect herself. She knew the pain of betrayal intimately and wanted to avoid it at all costs.

She might not completely trust him, but it was herself that she really doubted. Her own instincts were shit.

But she couldn't stay away from him. She didn't want to. These past few days with Brett had been amazing. He made her feel beautiful and perfect, something no one had ever managed to do.

Would it be wrong for her to embrace that sensation while she had it? Maybe later she'd regret the decision, but today she couldn't push him away.

Picking up her hand, Brett pressed it tight against his chest. Through the thin layer of his button-down shirt she could feel his racing heart. And even as he held her palm against the warmth of his body she found the erratic rhythm of her own heart matching his naturally.

"Do you feel what you do to me? Lexi, I couldn't fake that. Don't get me wrong, you're beautiful and I'm a conscious male. The rest of me would—and does— react whenever you're near. But this, this I've never felt before."

God, he was saying all the right things.

But that didn't mean they were true. Was she a chump because she wanted them to be? Or was she an idiot for hesitating?

It suddenly hit her. Either way, she could be losing. She'd spent so much of her life hesitating, afraid to make a mistake. Afraid to finally prove to everyone in her life just how unworthy and unlovable she really was.

But all that had gotten her was a life of expecting the worst. She was tired of the tension. Tired of waiting for the world to collapse and something bad to happen. Inevitably, it would. But in the meantime that expectation meant she couldn't enjoy the here and now.

And she wanted to enjoy every moment she had

with Brett. Already she knew there weren't going to be enough of them.

The idea of him leaving created a huge aching hole in the center of her chest. For the first time in her life she decided to take a page from Scarlett O'Hara's book and deal with that tomorrow.

It was time for her to take a chance.

Lexi took him by the hand and headed for the stairs. Without a word he followed.

Anticipation curled languidly through her belly. She could feel his cool blue eyes skating down her back to settle on her ass and she silently gave thanks to all the lunges she'd ever done to tighten her tushy. Effort well spent.

Unlike last night, when they reached her bedroom there was no overwhelming rush of heat. Brett stood silently at the foot of her bed watching her. But unlike before, when his motionless study had made her feel awkward and out of her element, today for some reason it made her feel wanted.

Maybe it was the intensity in his gaze, the way he looked at her, as if she was an oasis in the desert for a dying man.

At that moment, if he'd told her she was beautiful, Lexi might have actually believed him.

Late afternoon sunshine filtered through the windows. It bathed him in bright warmth. The first time they'd been together she hadn't seen all of him. The second time it had been too dark. Last night all she'd had space for was the rush of discovery.

Today she wanted to savor. To learn all the complexities of Brett—taste, touch, sound. So she could remember.

Slowly, she pulled his shirt up. Not bothering to unbutton it, she tugged it off over his head and dropped it to the floor. Lexi let her hands trail across his chest.

She enjoyed the sharp intake of breath when her nail grazed the flat disc of his nipple. The rough texture of hair as it scraped her palms. The smooth expanse of ribs and the valleys of his abs.

Her fingers swirled around the indentation of his belly button, discovering for the first time that he was ticklish there when he wheezed out and his muscles contracted from her touch. She followed the curving dip at his hip, trailing beneath the waistband of his jeans.

His hand wrapped around her wrist, stopping her from going farther. Through the shield of her lashes she frowned up at him. Bringing her palm up to his mouth, he nibbled there. She felt the caress at the base of her spine, a quickening knot of need.

His mouth trailed up her arm to the sensitive inside of her elbow. Never in her life had she thought of that spot on her body as erotic. But with Brett's lips there…

Not waiting for him to take her shirt off, Lexi pulled it over her head and threw it. One-handed, she flicked the clasp of her bra open and tore it away.

She wanted the moist heat of his mouth everywhere.

With deliberate care he covered every inch of her shoulder, across her collarbone and neck. His hands were busy while his mouth was occupied, making quick work of the zipper on her cotton shorts. They dropped from her hips to pool at her feet and she let them stay there. Who had time to care?

He picked her up and laid her across the bed. Cool sheets touched her skin and Lexi arched against them just for the feel. His blue-hot gaze caressed her, taking in every stretch of her body.

Never in her life had Lexi felt so decadent. Brett did that to her. He made her feel wanted, important and sensual.

The combination was intoxicatingly enticing.

His fingers trailed down the center of her body. Lexi bowed into his touch. The soft pressure of his lips picked up where they'd left off, trailing down her shoulder, arm and elbow to the center of her other palm. The knot pulled tighter.

He nipped at the pad of every finger, making each one tingle. When he reached her pinky he sucked it deep into his mouth and she gasped. The gentle tug of his mouth made her ache.

"You're killing me," she whispered, threading her fingers through the silky strands of his hair.

With hands and lips he worshipped her body, touching every inch of her except the places she wanted most. He ignored the begging peaks of her breasts and the throbbing core of her sex.

Blood pulsed frantically beneath her skin, and everywhere he touched she needed more. He'd awakened every cell in her body.

Lexi reached for the fly on his jeans. "I want to feel all of you." Strong fingers circled her wrist and stilled her fumbling attempt.

She whimpered, "Brett."

But she needn't have bothered because he was doing the job for her. The soft rasp of the zipper exploded through the room and when the swollen length of his sex sprang free she couldn't help but lick her lips.

Sharp eyes watched her tongue. And because she noticed his eyes narrowing at the gesture she did it again. His cock jerked and a clear bead of liquid pearled at the tip. Lexi arched, brushing her hips against him.

He fished several condoms from his pocket, scattering them across the bed before tossing the rest of his clothes to the floor.

"You planning on using all of those?" she asked, her voice deep and husky.

Naked skin to naked skin, his hardened body slid against her. His chest scraped nipples swollen with the need for his touch. Lexi groaned and everything inside her melted into a gooey mass of heat.

Bringing his lips close to her ear, he whispered, "Every. Single. One."

Oh, hell.

Lexi had never felt so alive or so adored. She was drowning in him, surrounded by Brett and everything he could make her feel.

It was too much. She wanted him to stop. She wanted the quick and dirty pleasure of the closet, not this emotionally charged moment that would leave her bare and devastated.

But it was too late.

How could he pull down every wall she'd ever built with nothing but his relentless caresses?

The hard length of him pressed against her hip. Without her telling it to, her body writhed beneath the weight of him, trying to bring them closer. As if that was possible.

She gasped for air. Begged for him. Thrashed beneath his weight.

The crinkling tear of foil made her suck in a hopeful breath. He lifted away, but only far enough that he could roll the latex down his length. But he didn't watch what he was doing. Instead, his eyes tangled with hers, light blue holding dark brown as he stared straight into her soul. Lexi tried to turn away, but she couldn't break the connection. Didn't really want to.

A knee nudged her thighs wide apart. Cool air touched the melted center of her sex.

And then he was there, pushing inside. Slowly. Patiently. Deliberately. He claimed her, more than any time before. He possessed every inch of her, inside and out.

Brett sank to the hilt, filling her as nothing else ever had.

She wrapped her hands around his hips, wanting to hold him to her. His sides labored, his ribs expanding and contracting with the strain of holding still.

But she didn't want him to hold still. Her internal muscles clenched around him, craving more.

Their bodies touched everywhere. His hard planes pressed against her soft curves. Lexi hadn't stopped long enough to realize just how perfectly they fit together. But she could feel it now, could feel all of him.

Lexi wanted him to move, to quench the agony of need he'd painstakingly built inside her. Instead, he waited, staying absolutely still so that she had no choice but to fall into the sensation of him surrounding her.

And she realized this was all she ever wanted. To relive this perfect moment with him over and over again, forever.

And then he was moving. Grinding his hips against her to get the last fraction of an inch out of their joining. Pulling out with the same exacting deliberation.

The rhythm he set drove her crazy. It built the pressure inside her to the screaming point. Her nails dug into his flanks, trying to urge him faster, but he refused to capitulate and free her from the delicious tension.

They were both a mass of raw nerves and need. Lexi couldn't breathe or think, all she could do was feel him and the way he worshipped her with his body.

Unexpected tears sprang to her eyes. She closed them to hide the reaction, but he stopped until she opened them again.

His hand scraped the hair from her face, anchoring at her nape. He brought them close, blocking out everything but her view of his wide blue eyes. Gone was the cool indifference, replaced by a burning intensity that scorched her.

Without breaking the connection of their stare, he quickened the pace and finally let her fall. But he was there to hold her.

Sensation swamped her, not just the release that slammed relentlessly through her, but the pain of vulnerability and the knowledge that she would never be the same. But she didn't care.

Not when he was staring just as relentlessly into her eyes. What she saw there scared the hell out of her—and made her want to weep with hope. For those few blazing moments she could believe she was everything. At least, to him.

And when he finally gave in to his own release she held on to him. Her arms wrapped around his chest and her hips pumped high for him. He called her name and the sound of it was the sweetest thing she'd ever known.

The tears she'd been holding back slipped down her cheeks. She buried her face in his neck, hoping he'd be too preoccupied to notice.

No one had ever made her feel as beautiful as he just had.

LEXI STRETCHED LANGUIDLY, a smile on her face before she'd even opened her eyes. Her hand smacked into something hard. And warm. Brett grunted, but a heavy arm snaked out and pulled her beneath him.

Sleepy blue eyes smoldered down at her. "Call in sick."

"I can't. My boss is a bitch."

The flat of his hand smacked down across the curve of her ass. Lexi yelped in surprise and jerked against him.

"I happen to like your boss and if you call her a bitch again I'm going to make you regret it."

Oh. He was playful today. It was a side of Brett she'd not seen very often. Intelligent, watchful, strong and capable. Sexy, smoldering. She'd seen all of those, but this was a new side of him. One she kind of liked.

Was it crazy that she didn't want last night to end? Without thinking about it, she found herself suggesting, "Why don't you come in with me today?"

Lexi didn't like anyone mucking around in her kitchen. Letting someone else in required her to turn over some of the responsibilities.

It also required her to trust.

But surprisingly, for the second day, she was hoping

to have company inside her little sanctuary. The other day had been good and she wasn't ready to let this end.

Brett pushed up onto his elbows, all trace of lazy somnolence gone. "Really?"

Maybe Brett was forcing her to turn over a new leaf, because the idea of having him there felt right.

"Why not?"

"I have some emails to return and a conference call later, but if I can use your office…"

Lexi smiled. She couldn't help it. He was upending his day so that he could spend it with her. Again. That made her feel special. And not quite as anxious about how vulnerable she'd been last night. "Sure."

Grabbing her waist, Brett rolled them both until she was draped across his chest. The sheets were a wreck around them. He'd made good on his promise and every one of the condoms he'd spread across her bed was gone. Her naked legs stuck out from beneath the covers. A single corner was wrapped around her hips and trailed precariously up her back.

Beneath her, he was blessedly naked. She could feel every inch of him. And he was definitely awake.

Scraping the hair back away from her face, he pulled her mouth to his and kissed her.

It was so easy to give in and fall beneath the wave of wanting him. The sensation was warm and comfortable, which surprised her. She was so used to being on edge around people that it was…a relief.

For the first time in a very long time she felt like she could really be herself. And that was something she hadn't let happen often, not even completely with her friends. The lessons she'd learned when she was younger had taught her to hide pieces of who she was. She didn't see it as a lie, but rather acceptance of the society she belonged to.

People conformed to all sorts of things.

Breaking their connection, Brett pulled away. A small, teasing smile played across his unbelievably beautiful mouth.

"Good morning, gorgeous."

His greeting took her by surprise. They'd been awake and talking for several minutes. But somehow it felt right. And more important than the mere words he'd just said.

As if there wasn't anywhere he'd rather be than right there with her.

Embarrassed that she was putting so much emphasis on an unimportant greeting, Lexi glanced away from him and caught a glimpse of the clock sitting beside her bed.

Pushing against his chest, she scrambled out of his hold.

"Get up, get up, get up. We're going to be late."

Brett followed her, a little more slowly. "I don't think it'll matter if you're a few minutes late unlocking the door, Lexi. You deserve five minutes now and then."

Sticking her head around the en suite door, she mumbled around her toothbrush. "I have a delivery of supplies showing up in twenty minutes."

He cocked his head and considered her. "Does that mean no time for a shower?"

The naughty gleam in his eyes gave him away, even if he did try to hide the intent.

Pointing a warning finger at him, Lexi tried to dissuade him. "Not the kind you're thinking. You can take one if you want. Alone. And meet me in a bit, but I'm walking out the door in five minutes with or without you."

Brett lunged for her. Lexi danced out of his grasp, threw her toothbrush back in the holder and sidestepped him to the closet.

"What happened to the woman who was twenty minutes late to dinner at your parents?"

Hopping on one foot, she jerked jeans up over her hips.

"That was different. This is business and if I'm not there it'll be days before I can get the delivery rescheduled. I need the supplies or I'll run out of product."

"You need to hire some help."

"Funny, I was thinking the same thing, but today that's not an option."

Brett stood in the doorway to her bathroom naked as the day he was born and completely oblivious and uncaring. Lexi couldn't help but stare at every mouthwatering inch of him. He was gorgeous, and for a little while he was hers.

"I'm trying to be good here, but if you keep looking at me that way you're going to miss more than your delivery."

Lexi shook her head, ducked back inside the closet and took a deep, steadying breath. Pressing her eyes closed, she tried to find her equilibrium, or her sanity, but apparently neither was available.

Instead, she settled for jerking a plain white shirt with little capped sleeves and a tapered waist over her head. She topped it with a red cardigan, adding a black rhinestone belt and red flats.

Coming out fully clothed was about her only hope of getting out of the house on time.

To her surprise, when she emerged Brett was dressed, as well. His hair was damp, tunnels from his fingers running through the dark strands, and he smelled like her vanilla body wash.

He headed into the kitchen first, grabbed the travel mug she kept ready by the coffeemaker and filled it from the waiting pot. In Lexi's life, one of the best inventions ever made had been the automatic timer on the coffeemaker.

Without bothering to ask, he opened her fridge, pulled out the gourmet creamer she had stashed in the door, splashed some inside, stirred and then handed it to her. Opening her cupboard, he grabbed her spare mug and made himself some to go.

Taking a sip, Lexi breathed in the healing power and waited for the caffeine to kick in.

And when it did something else hit her.

"How did you know the way I like my coffee?"

Brett glanced over his shoulder at her. "I don't know." Something on his face shifted and his eyebrows beetled. "I must have seen you."

"I guess." She couldn't remember having coffee in front of him, but maybe yesterday…

He'd paid attention to the way she preferred her coffee. That wasn't the gesture of a man only interested in sex, was it? Not that she had time to dwell.

Grabbing her keys off the kitchen counter, Brett bounced them in his hand and asked, "Are you ready?"

Lexi nodded.

This was very domestic. Too domestic.

Unease filled Lexi, but she refused to let it take hold. She wouldn't let it ruin the day before it had even gotten started. She was going to enjoy sharing the mundane morning tasks with him.

Last night had been about taking a risk, letting her guard down. What good would it do to put it back up in the bright light of day?

13

THE DAY WAS...unexpected. Brett watched as Lexi prepared all sorts of treats for her store. And when the baking and cooking were done she opened the front doors and single-handedly helped every customer who walked inside.

He was almost disappointed when he had to join in on a conference call with the project manager for a strip mall Bowen Enterprises was building in Texas. Bowen wanted some tweaks to the blueprints, none of them good. Brett resented the intrusion...and the reminder that he was in Sweetheart for something other than seducing the delectable chocolatier.

He much preferred watching Lexi as she greeted each customer by name, giving them the same dazzling smile that she shared with everyone—even the people who didn't deserve it. A scamp of a boy tried to swipe a cookie from the prepackaged display. Lexi caught him, pulled him by the collar into the corner and quietly lectured him on what he'd done wrong.

Instead of calling his parents—whom she obviously knew—or the sheriff to scare some sense into the boy, she looked at him with her warm chocolate eyes. Within minutes the poor boy was sobbing out how sorry he was and that he'd never do it again.

She hadn't even raised her voice.

Pulling the towel out of her waistband, she wiped his tearstained face, gave him one of the chocolate lollipops she'd made this morning and shooed him out the door.

Brett had no doubt the boy would think twice before trying to steal from anyone again, not just Lexi.

Where he'd come from, if anyone had caught him shoplifting he'd have been sent straight to juvie. In his neighborhood there were no second chances, which is why he'd worried so much about his little brother. Hunter had been headstrong and impulsive.

Sweetheart was a side of life that he'd never known. To his surprise, he realized that he'd kind of grown to like the place. And the people. Even when they'd been wary of him, they'd welcomed him anyway, giving him the benefit of the doubt.

It was late when the store finally emptied and the pace slowed. Even when there weren't customers, there had been work to do. And Brett realized he'd enjoyed being the one beside Lexi while she'd done it.

Lexi walked into the kitchen and slumped into a chair at the small table there. Brett slid behind her, wrapping his hands around her shoulders and rubbing.

She melted beneath his touch. He could feel each knot as it relaxed from her muscles. The contented hum that vibrated in her throat jolted through his own body, but he ignored the unmistakable signal. Now wasn't the time. She was exhausted.

"I wish you'd let me help more today. You really could have used it."

"I know, but it was faster just to do most of it myself."

"You should hire some help."

Her shoulders tightened again. Brett stayed silent, continued to rub and waited for her to relax again.

Finally, she sighed. "I know, but it's difficult to trust this place to anyone else."

Sweeping her hair over her shoulder, he revealed the bare skin at the nape of her neck. Leaning down, he placed his mouth just there and breathed against her skin. "Control freak."

He'd meant the words as a gentle rebuke, but instead they came out as a groan of need.

It had been a long day, watching her prance around in that tight little cardigan that did nothing to camouflage the luscious curves beneath, at least not now he knew they were there. He'd wanted to touch her all day. And now the place was empty.

But instead of falling in with his plan, Lexi slipped out from under his hold.

"Oh, no, you don't. I still have work to do."

Slowly, he let his eyes drag across her from the tip of her ponytail to the toe of her tiny red shoes. He'd always been more of a high-heel guy, but on Lexi those flats were sexy as hell.

And the apron. God, the apron. He wondered if she'd be willing to leave it on. It and nothing else.

In a husky voice, he asked, "What? I'll help. That way I can get my hands on you twice as fast."

Her skin flushed the most tempting shade of pink.

Her eyes sparkled and her tongue passed slowly across her parted lips.

"Underneath the display case you'll find boxes. Put everything in a separate container and make sure the lids are tight. I'll handle prep for tomorrow."

With a nod, he shot back into the front. With more speed than finesse, he managed to get all the leftovers boxed. Stacking them together, he clutched the tower of containers to his chest. They blocked his view, but he managed to find the curtain by feel and make it into the back without dropping a single one.

Sliding everything onto the table, he turned. Triumph raced just beneath his skin, but it didn't last. The vision that greeted him left him dumbstruck.

While he'd been gone Lexi had shed the sweater and popped open the first two buttons on her little white shirt. She'd taken down the ponytail, but replaced it with a messy knot at the top of her head. She hummed to herself, swaying her hips back and forth to a soundtrack only she could hear.

She looked amazing. Her skin glowed with happiness and health. Standing in front of the machine she'd told him was used to melt the chocolate and do something called tempering, he watched her lick a stray drop off of her finger.

Going after a drip on her forefinger, she put it in her mouth as far as it would go and sucked. Every muscle in his body clenched.

He groaned deep in his throat.

She yelped, spun and speared him with wide eyes. "I...I didn't realize you were there."

"Do it again."

She regained her equilibrium quickly. Too quickly for his taste. He liked her a little off-kilter. He liked knowing he could surprise her. She let so little fluster her.

"Do what again?"

"Lick chocolate off your finger."

Her pupils dilated as her eyes flared with heat. Slowly, she reached into the vat of chocolate behind her, dipped the tip of her finger into it and pulled it out. Opening her mouth, she sucked her finger deep inside. Her eyes closed for a moment as she savored the flavor of the chocolate.

But when they opened again, the smoldering glow was all for him. Slowly, she ran her tongue up the inside of her own finger. Beneath the tightness of his jeans, his cock throbbed.

He wanted her mouth on him.

Curling her still-wet finger at him, she beckoned him closer. And like a snake to the charmer, he went.

He stood before her, practically panting, waiting to see what she'd do next. She hadn't even touched him and he was burning for her.

"You're one of the sexiest women I've ever met, do you know that?"

She laughed, the sound low and mysterious. "I don't think anyone's ever told me that."

Maybe he was finally making progress because she didn't protest or tell him he was wrong.

Dipping her finger back into the reservoir, she pulled out a dollop. He expected her to offer it to him so that he could suck it off. Instead, with her other hand she tugged the collar of his shirt out of the way and smeared it up the side of his neck.

The chocolate was warm, but not hot. It was…thick and gooey. He could feel it rolling slowly down his skin. Until she leaned forward and with nothing but the quick tip of her tongue lapped it away.

Brett groaned. His hands clenched around her waist, but he didn't stop her.

"Mmm, you taste good."

"You're just saying that because you have a thing for chocolate."

He felt her smile more than saw it. "Probably. Maybe we should do it again to see."

She moved to grab more chocolate, but Brett stopped her.

Lexi looked up at him quizzically. "I've already contaminated this batch of chocolate. It'd be a shame to waste it."

In a gravelly voice, he croaked out, "We both know what a miserable failure our last experiment was."

"Does that mean you're ready to admit you lost our little bet?"

"Oh, I didn't lose." Brett leaned down, bit softly at her bottom lip before pulling it into his mouth to suck. "I got to touch you."

She tasted of chocolate and Lexi, an exhilarating combination he could seriously get used to.

An impish smile curved her lips. "I was pretty happy with the results myself."

"Good to know," he growled against her tempting mouth. "But I think we need a second opinion."

Reaching behind her, it was Brett's turn to dip into

the waiting vat. But he wasn't satisfied with a little skin. While one hand was in the chocolate the other made quick work of the buttons left on her shirt.

At the same time it popped open, he pulled out several fingers dripping with chocolate and spread them across her collarbone, through the valley between her breasts and over her ribs. Thick brown stripes decorated her entire torso. She looked like she'd been painted for war.

Looking bemusedly down at herself, she said, "That's a lot of chocolate."

"Good thing I'm hungry." Brett licked his lips. Lexi's gaze followed his every move.

She leaned back against the counter, her body bowing up, silently asking that he touch. Wrapping an arm around her waist, he pulled her higher, tight to his mouth.

The first taste of her exploded across his tongue. The chocolate was rich and smooth, just like her skin. But beneath it was something so uniquely Lexi. He'd come to think of her as sweet. Her scent, her taste, her personality. That was who she was.

But tonight, there was more. Something heady and satisfying. A pinch of spice and heat underlying everything.

He lapped at the chocolate, enjoying the way her breath caught when he sucked a particularly sensitive spot. Or the sigh of satisfaction when he pulled the cup of her bra away and stroked the flat of his tongue across the pebbled center of her breast.

The sticky treat was nothing more than a decadent wrapping hiding what he wanted most—her. And when the chocolate was gone he thought they were done with the game. But she had other plans.

"My turn," she said, making quick work of removing his shirt. Dipping into the chocolate, she spread it across his chest. Gooey clumps clung to the thin trail of hair across his belly. His stomach muscles seized when her talented fingers scraped across his nipple.

Up the side of his neck, across his ribs, the thick mess oozed across his skin. It was warm and...surprisingly pleasant. The chocolate cooled quickly, but he didn't care. Not when her mouth was busy nibbling at him.

With nimble fingers she unzipped his fly. Brett let out a hiss through clenched teeth when her fingers grazed across the distended length of his cock. She played, letting her fingers lightly trip up and down. The touch wasn't enough.

He wanted so much more. All of her. Everything she'd give him. And then he wanted more.

Brett wanted the connection they'd found last night. The complete lack of inhibition she'd gifted him with.

When she was near he could think of nothing else. Hell, even when she wasn't he was consumed by her. When had Lexi Harper become his own personal aphrodisiac?

She pushed his pants and boxers to the floor, kneeling in front of him to pull them off and away. Glancing up at him through lowered lashes, Lexi flashed the most wickedly sensual grin he'd ever seen.

Everything inside him stilled with anticipation. He wanted to find out what could follow such a shockingly debauched expression.

She reached behind her and Brett knew exactly what was coming.

The chocolate she anointed him with was a caress all its own. It was smooth and silky. Warm. She didn't just put a little on him, but coated his cock from base to tip, turning him into her own private chocolate-dipped treat.

Then she leaned down to suck. He wanted her to gobble him up, like a delight not even her legendary self-control could deny.

Instead she took just the very tip of him into the hot recesses of her mouth. When she pulled away Brett groaned. His hands tunneled into her hair, pulling out the band so that it could fall in a cloud around her face.

"I love your hair down."

"Mmm." The sound buzzed in the back of her throat and reverberated straight through his already throbbing groin.

The glossy strands of her hair twined around his fingers. The ends tickled his thighs.

With tiny licks, Lexi ran the tip of her tongue up his swollen length. Every time she reached the top, his cock kicked against her mouth, silently begging her to put him out of his misery.

But she ignored the request.

It felt as if it took forever. Brett wanted it to end. And he prayed it never would. Lexi was meticulous, careful to clean every last speck of rich chocolate off his skin.

By the time most of it was gone he was panting and every muscle in his body was strung hard. His hands, still tangled in her hair, trembled.

Rolling her eyes up at him, she watched him through

lowered lashes. The tiniest smudge of chocolate peeked out of the corner of her mouth.

It was the sexiest thing he'd ever seen. And he couldn't take any more.

Grasping her, he laid her out flat across the stainless-steel surface of her work counter.

Lexi sucked in a shocked breath when her naked skin connected with the cool surface. She leaned toward him and Brett took advantage, snagging the distended tip of a nipple between his starving lips.

Brett fished a condom out of the pocket of his discarded pants, then tore the rest of her clothes from her body. And when he finally touched her he found her sex wet, swollen and so ready for him.

Sheathing himself in latex, he grasped her hips and held her still so he could slide home. Her body welcomed him, stretching to take everything he could give her.

She sighed, not with the heated frenzy he'd expected, but a soft sound of relief and recognition. Lexi reached for him, pulling him down so their bodies slid languidly against each other.

He enjoyed the moment and the throbbing heat of her wrapped tight around him. Their bodies were sticky, clinging together. They were reluctant to let go of each other.

But the pressure to move and feel was too much and quickly overwhelmed him. He needed her. Now.

Pushing her knee up, Brett opened her up so he could give her more. Slowly, he pulled out and just as deliberately slipped back in. Lexi's eyes closed in ecstasy and her head rolled backward against the table, exposing her throat.

Brett's mouth trailed down the open invitation, latching on to the fluttering pulse. He sucked. Her internal muscles clamped tighter around him.

He pushed them both. In and out. Over and over. Slowly driving the pace until they were both delirious. Beneath him Lexi bucked. She tried to force him to go faster, but his palm flat against the table beneath her knee kept her prisoner.

She whimpered. And quivered. Every muscle in her body went rigid. And then she was screaming his name.

Her body pulsed around him, wave after wave of her relentless release begging him to join her. And he couldn't hold back. Not anymore.

The knot at the base of his spine expanded. And exploded.

The entire world went dark. Bursts of light, red, blue, green and gold, shot through the inky blackness.

The next thing Brett knew, he was lying beside Lexi on the cool surface of the table.

Her body was curled into his, tucked against his side, her head burrowed into his shoulder. The moist heat of her breath tickled across his chest. Her fingers were threaded through his chest hair, resting right over his heart.

Every few seconds her body would shudder.

He might have thought her cold, except her skin still burned wherever he touched.

Finally, when full use of his brain had returned, he mumbled, "That was hot."

Pushing against his chest, Lexi looked down at

him, a tiny frown arrowing between her brows. "No, it wasn't. I turned the chocolate down. It should have only been warm."

Brett buried his face into the cloud of her hair and tugged her down so their noses touched. He stared into the deep pool of her chocolate eyes. Every time he saw them now he'd think of this day. And just what she could do with that decadent delight.

"I meant you."

"Oh," she said, rolling down until their lips touched softly. "That's the most chocolate I've eaten since I was a kid."

"That's…" Sad was what he wanted to say, but settled for "…wrong."

She shrugged. Dropping back down onto his chest. He liked her there, but now he couldn't look into her eyes.

"There's nothing wrong with indulging, Lexi."

"Sure, as long as you know when to stop."

His fingers played softly in her hair. Several of the strands were covered in streaks of chocolate, but he didn't say anything. If he did she'd get up and he didn't want that.

"You don't think you'd know when to stop?"

Her head rolled against him in a silent confession. "I have no willpower. Not when it comes to chocolate." Slowly, her eyes lifted to his. "And apparently you."

14

THEY SNUCK UP the walkway to the inn like two drunken teenagers returning after curfew, unable to smother their laughter. Lexi had never been one to break the rules, so it was something she hadn't actually done. Her parents had been through hell when Gage was a teenager, and Lexi's sole mission in life had been to not add to the trouble.

Surprisingly, she had to admit the adrenaline and joy carried some appeal. Although she and Brett weren't breaking any rules, they were definitely trying to get inside without being caught.

They were both sticky. Their clothes were in disarray and somehow Brett's pants had a streak of chocolate slashing straight across the fly. Lexi's blond hair had more than a few globs of dried chocolate.

Her skin was flushed and her eyes sparkled. If anyone saw them there'd be no denying what they'd been doing. And if anyone saw them like this the entire town would know about it by morning.

She'd suggested showering at her store, but Brett had refused. He'd convinced her that the shower in his room

was bigger—big enough for two when hers definitely
wasn't. He needed new clothes anyway. And he'd per-
suaded her with kisses and touches until any thought
of protesting had fled from her mind. Before she'd realized what was happening, the store was locked and
they were creeping up the back porch.

A stair creaked. Brett shushed her with a mock glare.

They opened the door and stared into Mrs. McKinnon's menacing glower. Her arms were crossed over her
chest and her foot tapped unhappily against the worn
boards of her hardwood floor.

"You two are worse than my kids and grandkids
combined."

Even close to seventy, Mrs. McKinnon's eyesight was
still sharp enough to rake across them both. She didn't
miss a single detail of their disheveled state.

Lexi should be mortified. But she wasn't. She should
be cringing that the grapevine was about to heat up
with her latest escapade. But she couldn't seem to care.

Maybe she should indulge in chocolate-covered sex
more often. It definitely mellowed her.

"Do not ruin my nice clean sheets, Alexis Harper. If
you want to make a mess of someone's bed, why don't
you do it at your own house?"

Brett's arm wrapped around her waist and he pulled
her hard against the shelter of his body.

"We have no intention of ruining anything, Mrs.
McKinnon."

She sniffed her skepticism. "See that you don't."

Throwing a sheepish grin over his shoulder, Brett
tugged on their joined hands and walked past Mrs.
McKinnon.

Lexi had never really been inside the guest rooms at the inn. Occasionally she'd been to a tea or bridal shower on the main floor, but since she lived here she'd never needed to stay. And, honestly, she hadn't ever really thought about the inn and how it served the community.

She was always busy running her own business.

Looking around the room, Lexi frowned. It was cramped. Stuffed to the gills with furniture. All the pieces were antique and held a charming kind of history, but the space lacked the ease of movement that modern hotel rooms usually had.

The thought of a small family with two adults and a child or two trying to share the space made her cringe.

When she looked up at Brett, she realized he was watching her with that same shrewd, sharp gaze she recognized from the first night. She waited for him to say something, but when he did it wasn't what she'd expected.

"Are you coming?"

He disappeared inside the bathroom. The sound of rushing water filled the space. She was sticky, her hair was a mess and a sexy, naked man had just beckoned her to get wet. She'd never wanted anything more in her life.

Happiness swelled inside her chest. Maybe, just maybe, this was going to work out. He wouldn't break her heart…

The thought trailed away to nothing. Break. Her. Heart. The organ stuttered painful inside her chest. It squeezed, forcing all of the blood through her body in a flooding surge that left her lightheaded.

In order for him to break it, that meant he had to hold it.

The gentle hum of Brett's voice floated out to her. The deep rumble wrapped around her. He'd started singing. And he was awful, every note slightly off-key.

How could she love this man and not know that he couldn't sing? How could she have let herself fall in love with him?

Maybe the real question was how could she have stopped?

Her legs shook. Taking a few halting steps, Lexi walked to the doorway and looked inside. She could just make out the dark outline of his body against the frosted glass.

Even hazy, he was beautiful. But there was more to Brett than a rough-hewn form that could leave any woman breathless and wanting. He was sexy, intelligent, dedicated and a meticulous lover. She'd been surprised by the sweet side she'd gotten a few glimpses of, although she wasn't sure why. Especially after hearing how much he cared for and protected his mother and brother.

What was she going to do?

Lexi swallowed a heavy lump that caught in her throat.

Nothing. What could she do? They'd only just met. It was way too soon to hit him with her shocking revelation. He wasn't ready to hear the big *L* word, even if she had been ready to tell him. And she wasn't.

In a few weeks he'd leave and head back to Philadelphia. She'd cross the bridge of what to do when that happened. Maybe they could start slow, a long-distance relationship. She'd never tried that.

Feeling better, a little more centered, Lexi shed her clothes and joined him in the shower. Hot steam billowed around them and it was easy to bury her nervous energy beneath the heat he stirred in her.

Later, squeaky clean, her skin pink and pruney from staying too long in the water, she curled up on his bed. Wrapped in a fluffy robe, she watched him as he messed with a laptop open on the desk. Something that Hope had said several days ago blasted through her brain.

"Show me the drawings you're working on." She'd shared her business and her passion for baking with him. She wanted to know what had drawn him to architecture. To understand.

Startled, Brett threw a look at her over his shoulder. He studied her for several seconds and then nodded.

He opened a program as she walked across to stand behind him. Her fingers curled around the spindled back of his chair, but didn't stay there long. Not with the temptation of his damp hair so close. Lexi threaded her fingers into the thick strands at his nape.

His fingers tapped against the keyboard. She was so distracted by touching him that it took her several seconds to realize his shoulders were tense. Was he nervous about showing her?

Shifting, Brett set his hands on her hips and pulled her around until she was facing him. He didn't let her go, but settled her against the edge of the desk and studied her face.

That same sharp, careful and calculated expression

she'd seen the night they'd met was back. For some reason, it made her nervous.

"Sweetheart needs this resort, Lexi."

She made a sound in the back of her throat. A week ago it would have been stronger, an unmistakable dissent, but now she wasn't entirely certain what to think. She knew her friends were considering Brett's arguments.

"It'll be good for business. Good for Sugar and Spice. It'll increase capacity during peak seasons and be a draw during off seasons."

Through the soft fabric of her robe his thumbs rubbed tiny, distracting circles against her hips.

"Maybe."

He frowned. Turning his attention back to the computer, his fingers scrolled across the touchpad and a set of drawings popped up onto the screen.

Lexi leaned forward, trying to make sense of what she was looking at. He tumbled her into his lap, drawing her closer. It didn't help much; she still didn't understand exactly what they meant.

"What's this?"

Another window opened, a full-color drawing popping up onto the screen. And she gasped.

"Something I've been working on."

It was the resort. Only it was so much better than what Bowen had originally submitted. And what Brett had originally designed.

"This is…gorgeous." And it was. Elegantly rustic. Lexi could just imagine sunlight glinting off the water and reflecting off the soaring wall of windows. "Why didn't you submit this the first time? These plans might have gotten approved."

She couldn't see him, but she could hear the frustration in his voice when he answered. "Because this isn't the design my boss wanted."

"But this is what Sweetheart needs."

"I know." His hands smoothed up and down her arms. "I'm trying, Lexi. But Bowen is a stubborn man and my job is to get the resort built."

She twisted, wanting to look in his eyes. "Why are you fighting so hard for this? It's obvious you realize how terrible Bowen's plans are."

Brett set her on her feet. He stood and paced away, scraping a hand through his hair. The still-damp strands stood on end. She might have found the sight funny if his agitation hadn't been so obvious. Watching his cool, calm facade crack just a little made her heart lurch painfully in her chest.

"When the plans are approved I get a bonus." He stole a quick glance at her from beneath long, inky lashes, but quickly turned away again.

"I need that money, Lexi. I've been trying to open my own firm for years, saving every penny I can. But it's taken me longer than I hoped. I've had to dip into my nest egg a couple times, for tuition, moving my mom to a better neighborhood. Good choices, but still…this bonus gives me the large influx of cash I need to break from Bowen."

He tried to hide the disgust when he said Bowen's name, but Lexi heard it in his voice anyway.

"You don't like him," she said, a combination of surprise and consternation stealing her breath.

His mouth twisted. "Not really."

"Brett, if you don't want to work for him why do you want us to work with him?"

A hand brushed over his face, pushing up and down as his eyes screwed tight.

"Is it just about the money?"

His eyes popped open and he speared her with a sharp gaze. "You know me better than that."

"Do I?" she countered. She thought she had, but now she was beginning to wonder.

Frustration stiffening every movement, Brett yanked several glossy folders from a stack and thrust them at her.

"I'm trying to find the only way through a minefield, Lexi. Sweetheart needs the resort. Bowen already owns the land. I know him, he's a bulldog when he gets his teeth sunk into a bone and he wants this. He'll find a way, somehow, to get what he wants. He always does.

"He sent me those. Dossiers on every member of the town council. On your family."

"On me," she breathed out, staring down at her own face smiling back at her through the clear plastic cover.

"Yes, on you. That's the way Bowen works, but it isn't the way I work. I'm not interested in playing dirty or extorting cooperation."

Lexi swallowed, hard. She opened the slick cover. Each page she turned made her cringe even more. Details of her life. Her elementary school grades. A medical report from the clinic she'd used while she was in culinary school.

Anger slammed through her. Wasn't that kind of information supposed to be confidential? Apparently not. Not for Brett Newcomb and Bowen Enterprises.

There were pictures. Some of them snapshots she recognized from her friend's social media sites. One in particular caught her attention. Her face was framed by the fuzzy hood of the jacket she'd worn while she was in Switzerland, the Alps rising behind her as she stared into the inviting lens of the camera.

Switzerland. She *hadn't* told him about that trip. He'd known about it from the information he'd been fed. Along with the way she preferred her coffee and God only knew what else.

The amount of information was staggering and unsettling.

"How did he get this?" She shook the dossier. Pages on her life fluttered accusingly between them.

"I don't know. I didn't ask."

Her skin flushed with the force of her anger. She glared at Brett, unsure who she was more pissed at—him or herself. She'd let her guard down, trusted him.

"But you read it."

"Yes. No. Yes, but not the way you think. Not because I wanted to use the information to seduce you."

Lexi scoffed at his explanation. Her hands trembled. "Please, that's exactly what you did."

God, the details about her struggle with her weight and her self-image issues were practically a road map for what to say and do to win her trust. And she'd fallen for it.

Again.

When would she learn?

He'd lied to her. That first night she'd asked him if

he'd known who she was when he bought the cake. Obviously, the real answer had been yes. He'd known full well she was the mayor's daughter and flirted with her to get what he wanted.

And it wasn't just about the resort…he had personal reasons. Lexi's stomach rolled. The heavy ball of chocolate twisted deep inside her. It suddenly hit her. He'd slept with her for money.

Plenty of people had made her feel useless and unimportant in her life, but Brett took the prize for making her feel cheap.

How could he do this? Last night had meant nothing to him. She'd been laying herself bare, stripping away all of her barriers and he'd been deceiving her the entire time.

Tears, hot and weak, stung the backs of her eyes. She refused to shed them in front of him.

Refused to let him see just how much he'd hurt her. She did have some pride left.

In one quick motion, Lexi snatched up her purse and bolted for the door. She'd heard enough.

DAMMIT! BEFORE HE'D realized what she meant to do, Lexi was out the door. From across the room, he couldn't catch her in time. And not even pointing out that she was in nothing but a bathrobe had stopped her.

Skidding across the hardwood of the entryway, Brett clamored out onto the front porch just in time to see her SUV peel out of the parking lot. Swearing again, he wasted precious time running back upstairs for the keys to his rental car and a shirt. He was less than five minutes behind her, but her little cottage was completely dark when he arrived and her car wasn't in the driveway.

That didn't stop him from pounding on the door and rattling the hinges anyway. His heart thudded unsteadily inside his chest.

Lexi wasn't the first woman he'd ever pissed off. But she was first one whose anger mattered. He didn't want her furious with him. He didn't want her walking away without at least letting him explain.

And now that he knew about her history…of course that report would feel like the worst betrayal. Would put everything he'd said and done in the worst possible light. If he'd been thinking clearly he never would have given it to her. But he'd wanted her to understand that he was trying to find the best way to make everyone happy…and failing miserably at it.

Until faced with the possibility of losing her, Brett hadn't realized just how terrifying the prospect would be. He no longer gave a damn what happened with the resort. He cared about getting Lexi back.

She had to at least listen.

Where was she?

Maybe she'd gotten into an accident. She'd peeled out of the parking lot spitting gravel. Driving while enraged and distracted could get her killed.

Brett paced restlessly across her front porch. Or maybe she'd run to her parents. Or brother.

He nervously bounced the keys in his hands, trying to decide what to do. Should he leave and try to find her or wait for her to return?

He wasn't used to uncertainty and the longer he

stewed and stalked the easier it was to turn his anxiety into anger and point it directly at her.

She'd walked away.

Just like his dad. The thought was a lightning bolt out of the blue. Brett hadn't thought of his dad in years. It was wasted energy and he'd learned long ago that wishing for something unattainable only led to disappointment.

Although Lexi's flight away had little in common with that situation. His dad had been a selfish bastard who didn't care about anyone but himself. Brett had been nine when he disappeared. No phone calls. No Christmas cards.

When he was eighteen, a freshman in college, Brett had gotten up the courage to find him. He'd scraped together a little money and hired a private investigator. He'd needed to know. For himself and for Hunter.

He'd expected to find nothing more than a grave somewhere. Instead, he'd discovered a middle-aged man with a good job, a nice family and a house that wasn't crumbling.

Brett had been so angry. And then hurt and betrayed.

That same combination of emotions snaked inside him, a poisonous mixture that he didn't like and never wanted to experience again.

He was about to leave, *screw this* echoing ominously through his head, when Lexi's SUV pulled into the drive. From his vantage point in the shadows of her porch, he watched her approach.

Somewhere she'd found some clothes, probably from Sugar & Spice. She moved slowly, picking her way up the path. She silently studied him, her deep brown eyes distant and wary. She paused at the bottom of the steps, her hand wrapped around the post of her porch.

She was waiting for any reason to bolt.

"You can't just leave, Lexi." His voice was harsher than he'd expected. It was filled with every ounce of betrayal and hurt that he didn't want to feel and didn't want her to hear. "You need to listen to me."

Her mouth tightened and she tossed the long tail of her beautiful blond hair over her shoulder. "I don't need to do anything, Brett."

The bright lick of anger heated her eyes for the briefest moment before it was extinguished, replaced by the damnable mask of indifference she'd perfected. But not even she could deny the flush that flamed up her skin.

Brett took a step towards her. She moved back.

"It's pretty obvious you got what you wanted."

Her knuckles tightened on the post. Brett could see the white ridge of them and his stomach rolled.

"You're right, I got exactly what I wanted. You, Lexi. Until tonight have I mentioned the resort to you? Have I tried to change your mind? Have I asked you to speak to your father?"

Slowly, she shook her head. But he could see in her expression that the admission wasn't enough. Her wary hesitation cut deep. Brett's back teeth ground together.

"You fascinate me, Lexi. You're such a puzzle. Sweet and giving and sexy as hell. You…don't make sense."

Her eyes widened and her body fell backward as if his words had hit her square in the chest.

"No, that's not what I mean. I'm used to logical. Easy. In my life things are what they appear. And it's easier that way. I know exactly what to expect. There are no surprises."

Brett's voice dropped low. The words were rough when they exited his raw throat. "I don't like surprises, Lexi. They're not usually good. I read the dossier because I wanted to know everything I could about you.

"That first day, I was intrigued when I walked into your store. I was impressed with the way you handled that witch…and me. And then at your parents'…I couldn't forget the image of you crouched in front of me in that tiny black dress trying to clean chocolate off my shoes. When Bowen sent me the info the next morning I couldn't resist."

"You didn't know who I was at first?"

"I already told you I didn't."

"But now I don't know what to trust, Brett. What was truth and what was a lie."

Brett growled low in his throat, frustration getting the better of him. "Lexi, I didn't lie to you about that."

Slowly, she shook her head. "You need to leave." Her words were cold, but he could hear the hurt beneath them. He could see it in the way her shoulders slumped forward and her arm wrapped protectively around her waist.

Slowly, he walked forward. The echo of his shoes against the worn boards was the only sound between them.

Stopping, Brett looked straight into her eyes. He reached for her, running a single finger down the slope of her jaw. Lexi pulled back, but she didn't drop her gaze.

Instead, she let him see just how shaken and upset

she was. The force of her emotions slammed into him, overwhelming him. He didn't know what to do with them.

Finally, she whispered, "We both knew this couldn't last. Maybe it's better this way."

He knew he should agree, but he didn't want to. But what argument could he make?

Tangling his fingers in her hair, he pulled her to him. She resisted, her neck stiffening to try and hold them apart, but he wouldn't let her. If he'd known tonight was the last time he would touch her, he would have paid more attention, given her more pleasure, made more memories.

Bringing their mouths close, he kissed her. The heat that was always there flashed between them. Lexi gasped and opened for him. There was a bitter edge to the kiss, a sadness that he didn't want to think about or examine.

Both of them panted and still he pulled away, leaving her with one thing to remember. For her sake, he hoped she believed him.

"This had nothing to do with the resort."

15

SHE DIDN'T BELIEVE him. She wanted to, but that almost made it worse. She was such a naive idiot. When would she learn?

Men like Brett Newcomb didn't want her for herself. How could they?

Lexi tried not to let it hurt, but of course it did. She tried not to let the hurt show, but she couldn't even manage that.

No stranger to pasting on a smile and pretending, she went through the motions for a couple of days. But her friends noticed. Willow dropped by and asked her where Brett was. No one had seen him around town. Apparently, when he'd left her house, he'd also left Sweetheart.

Lexi wasn't entirely certain what to make of that. Not that it really mattered. Brett was gone and somehow she had to find a way to get over it. Over him.

But it hurt. Much more than learning Brandon had used her. With Brandon her pride had been damaged. Brett had crushed her heart.

Three days after Brett disappeared, Hope showed up

at Sugar & Spice's back door. They fell into the normal routine, Lexi pulling out a container of lemon bars stashed beneath the counter.

Her friend was surprisingly quiet today, sitting at the table and munching in silence. Her eyes were heavy on Lexi's back as she dipped apples into a large vat of caramel.

Lexi fought the need to squirm under her friend's scrutiny. Hope saw too much and knew her better than just about anyone, which made keeping up the charade difficult.

Finally her friend said, "I'm here."

Lexi shot a quick glance over her shoulder and then returned to the safety of her work. "I know."

"No. I'm here. Whenever you want to talk about it."

"Nothing happened."

Disbelief buzzed in the back of Hope's throat.

Lexi slammed an apple down onto the wax paper a little harder than she'd intended. "We had sex. I found out he was pushing the resort for a huge amount of money. And that he had a fat dossier with information on me, including my elementary school grades and my medical records from New York. He left."

Hope whistled low under her breath. "That asshole. Didn't see that one coming."

Neither had she. That was the problem. She should have. Unlike with Brandon, Brett had told her exactly who he was and why he was in town. He'd made no attempts to hide his ulterior motives. And still she'd fallen for him. Hard.

"Brandon used me."

Hope's mouth twisted. "No one likes to be used."

"But I got over it. I mean, what I worried about more than anything was him printing what I'd told him about Gage, but when that didn't happen I stopped worrying."

"This is different," Hope said, the words a statement not a question.

Slowly, Lexi nodded. She didn't want it to be different. She didn't want to walk into her little cottage, her private sanctuary for the past several years, and fight disappointment because she knew he wouldn't be there. She didn't want to catch herself watching the sidewalk outside her store, hoping that he might be there.

She didn't want to wait for him to come back. Because that wasn't going to happen. She'd told him to go and he'd left.

Sure, after she'd calmed down and thought about what he'd said, some of his statements had rung true. No, he'd never asked her to intervene with her dad or the town council. But that could just be because she'd beaten him to the punch.

"I mean, I knew when we started this that it wasn't going to be hearts and flowers. I'm not stupid. The council has no intention of approving the rezoning or permits. Eventually he'd have left and moved on to another project. My store is here. His job is somewhere else. It wasn't like we had a future."

Lexi felt the burn of tears. She hated herself for the weakness, but couldn't stop it. To cover it up, she began flinging apples into the caramel with more force than finesse. Which wasn't like her. She prided herself on the quality of her product.

Hope's hand settled over her own, stalling the haphazard process. Lexi looked down at the mess she'd made. Ribbons of caramel trailed across the floor, counter and tray. It spread like a molten pool beneath the apples she'd just ruined.

"Fudge," she said, the single word choking in the back of her throat.

Her friend settled her hip against the counter, pulling both of her hands into her grasp and forcing her to turn and look at her.

"You're in love with him?"

Hope stared at her. Her friend's eyes were filled with compassion and it was her complete undoing.

Silent tears slid over the edge, tracking down her face as she nodded.

Hope enveloped her in the comforting hug she desperately needed. Guiding her across to the table, Hope pressed her into a chair. She handed her a cold bottle of water and one of the lemon bars.

"Eat."

Lexi tried to protest, but Hope wouldn't hear it.

"You look like you've lost five pounds in the last few days."

Which didn't really surprise Lexi, since not even chocolate had been appetizing. She'd barely eaten anything, forcing herself to sample her product for no other reason than testing its quality.

Her relationship with Brett was affecting her work, which was something that had never happened before. In the past, baking and cooking had been her refuge, where she could be alone and find peace.

But he'd even taken that. Her kitchen reminded her of him. Her store reminded her of him. Hell, even her treadmill reminded her of him. Brett had taken all of her coping mechanisms and smashed them to bits.

So that Hope would stop hovering, Lexi forced herself to chew and swallow. The pastry was good. She was objective enough to taste the complex flavors that burst across her tongue. The crust was light and flaky. And the lemony treat turned to a solid ball in her stomach the minute she swallowed.

God, she was a mess.

"What are you going to do?"

Lexi grimaced. "I'm going to get through today, go home, go to bed, get up and do it all again tomorrow."

Hope frowned. "I meant about Brett."

"Nothing."

"Nothing?"

"What exactly do you think I should do, Hope? Run after him? Why? It wouldn't change anything. He used me. And even if he didn't, it was a fling. An affair. And it's over."

The creases across Hope's forehead deepened. She opened her mouth, but Lexi cut her off.

"I'll be fine, Hope. I knew it would end. I'm not going to deny that it hurts, but eventually, I'll get over it."

Maybe if she said it enough, one day she'd be able to make the promise a reality.

BRETT WAS UTTERLY at a loss. He'd been home for a week, but his nice, modern apartment no longer felt right.

Driving out of Sweetheart had bothered him—more than he'd ever expected. In the short time he'd been there he'd come to appreciate the place.

He'd miss the people. Even the nosy Mrs. McKinnon. Maybe especially her. There was a sense of belonging that he'd never found anywhere else and now that he was gone, he noticed the loss. Hell, he didn't even know his neighbor's names. That had never struck him as strange before Lexi, but it did now.

Brett wasn't entirely certain when the plan had begun to form. Perhaps it had been a kernel rolling around in the back of his brain for days, waiting to pop fully formed to the forefront on the flight home. Either way, he knew exactly what he had to do—for Sweetheart, himself and Lexi.

He was not looking forward to his upcoming conversation with Bowen, but there was nothing for it. Everything hinged on whether or not he could get his boss on board.

Setting his laptop into the docking station, he settled back into the desk that had been his for years. Firing up his machine, he opened the redesigned plans he'd been working on at the inn.

The excitement he felt was hard to dismiss. These plans were so different from the first drafts. There was pride, an emotion he hadn't really experienced in a while when thinking about his work. When had he lost that?

He stared at the bold lines of the drawings. He hoped what he was about to do would convince Lexi that the resort had nothing to do with what they had. But even if it didn't, he wouldn't regret the decision he'd made. It was the right thing to do—for everyone.

He just needed a bank to agree and accept the seed

money he had put aside as a down payment on some prime lakeside real estate.

Assuming he could talk his boss into selling.

TWO WEEKS AFTER Brett left, Lexi walked into the town hall for another meeting. The building was older, built in the early fifties. It probably could have done with a face-lift. The facade was nice enough, but there were still cracks, peeling paint, broken fixtures and chipped linoleum.

After a long day at the shop, she was exhausted, and would rather be at home, but her dad had asked her to come so...

The low rumble of voices drifted up the stairs from the basement, greeting her. She descended into the wide-open space and what looked like the entire adult population of Sweetheart.

She hadn't asked what was on the agenda, but maybe she should have. Large crowds usually meant something controversial, but no one had mentioned anything to her.

Lexi moved through the crowd, smiling and passing out generic pleasantries as she went. Her goal was the front of the room where her dad would be preparing to start the meeting, but she didn't make it.

The loud boom of her father's voice rose above the buzz. "Would everyone take their seats?"

General shuffling ensued. Out of the crowd some-one grasped her elbow. When she turned, Lexi real-ized it was Hope. Greeting her, Hope patted the open seat beside her.

Lexi sank down and then almost immediately popped

back up. At the front of the room, Brett Newcomb stood talking to her father.

Her heart stilled and then began to race. Her body flushed hot and then went icy cold.

"What is he doing here?" she hissed at Hope.

As if he'd sensed her scrutiny, Brett's gaze jerked up and somehow managed to zero in on hers. She felt the punch of his cool blue gaze straight to the center of her soul. Her mouth went dry. Without realizing what she was doing, her tongue darted out to lick across parched lips. And heat kindled deep inside his eyes.

But then he looked away, taking all the warmth with him. Lexi fought against the feeling of being dismissed. Unneeded and unwanted.

Clenching her jaw, she shifted in her seat. He wasn't there for her. If he had been then he would have let her know he was back in town.

It was well and truly over. Lexi wasn't certain why that realization had surprised her, considering she hadn't spoken to Brett in weeks. But it did. Until that moment she hadn't realized she'd been harboring a hope that he'd come back for her.

Instead, he was here for the resort, reinforcing everything she'd thought about his intentions in the first place.

"We're suspending our regular agenda tonight to focus on a request for rezoning that's been brought before the council."

Brett stood tall and silent at the front of the room, an expensive and impressive business suit highlighting his beautiful body. He looked amazing. And Lexi wanted to leave, but she couldn't do it now without making a scene.

Something she'd avoid at all costs. Most everyone in this room knew—or thought they knew—what had happened between her and Brett. She would not give them any more grist for the mill.

So she was stuck, staring at the screen erected behind Brett and her father instead of at the man himself. A logo she'd never seen bounced around the blank white background—Sweet Heart Consortium, with the heart made of two entwined letters she couldn't identify.

A hush fell over the room as the lights dimmed. Brett stepped forward. The logo disappeared and a beautiful rendering of a building popped into its place.

Lexi gasped. She recognized it. It was the same computer-generated drawing he'd shown her that last night. Several people around her clapped. Brett waved his hand as if to silence everyone.

The design was just as perfect as she remembered. All rustic browns with pops of blue and green. The structure blended into the surroundings, using banks of windows to reflect back the setting around it.

Large pines and oaks towered behind the rendering. The lake sparkled. And the blue sky was drenched in sunlight. This resort looked sophisticated, integrated and relaxing.

How had he convinced Bowen to accept the design?

She listened silently as Brett clicked through slide after slide. He showed detailed architectural drawings and talked about green technology. Romantic touches. Providing space for both couples and families. Expanding their brand to cater to different clienteles at different times of the year.

Lexi listened, but her brain had hit saturation point and she was having trouble taking it all in.

Brett's presentation ended. The logo appeared again on the screen, bouncing lazily. The lights popped back on and he stood at the front of the room, his feet planted wide and his hands loose at his sides.

He appeared completely relaxed. At ease with being in front of the crowd and presenting this new concept to everyone.

But she knew better. She could see the tension in the tight lines that bracketed his mouth, the vein that pulsed just beneath his jaw.

"I'm happy to answer any questions."

One of the council members inquired about the expected timeline.

"That depends on approval and funding. By our calculations, construction could take anywhere from nine to twelve months after we break ground."

A single question kept bouncing around her brain, just like the logo behind Brett. "What's this consortium? What happened to Bowen?"

His cool gaze swung to hers. He paused for several moments. The dark edge of his tongue swept across the tempting surface of his bottom lip.

"Bowen is out."

"What do you mean?"

"He sold the land."

Lexi's gaze searched his. There was something he wasn't saying. She could see the hesitation deep inside his eyes.

"To who?"

He swallowed. Lexi watched the smooth column of his throat with fascination. His skin brightened with a flush of heat. He was nervous.

The realization startled Lexi. Nothing flustered Brett Newcomb. He was always confident and coolly in control.

"Me."

She stared at him, silent and dumbfounded.

"How?" How had he been able to afford that? The land was prime real estate.

With a negligent shrug that seemed completely out of place, he answered, "I had some money. And took out a huge loan."

Was she the only one who could see the slick edge of fear lurking deep in his eyes? He'd used the money he'd been saving. The nest egg he'd spent years building. Why in heaven's name would he give up that security?

She stared at him, unable to process just what that meant.

"I've purchased the land, but I'm going to need the support of other investors to make the resort feasible. A consortium of private owners. I know this town is full of savvy business owners. In the last few weeks I've had a chance to speak to quite a few of you. Not only will there be an opportunity for a return on your investment when the resort opens, but opportunities to cross-promote your other businesses."

Money. Of course, that's what all this was about. Brett had seen an opportunity and had taken a calculated risk. Lexi had to admit it was a good one.

With the new designs, she couldn't see how the venture could fail.

That's why he'd come back. Not for her.

And now she'd have to see him around town. God, it hurt. Lexi's body curled inward, protecting herself in the only way she could.

She'd figure out a way to deal with this, but not today. Today it was too much and she needed to get out of here before she lost it and made a fool of herself in front of the entire town.

Standing suddenly, Lexi tried to slip out quietly, but it didn't work. She wasn't even halfway down the aisle when the smooth, even tone of Brett's voice stopped her. "Don't leave."

Lexi paused, but she didn't turn. She didn't trust herself to look at him and not fall apart.

"Lexi." His voice was rough, cracking halfway through her name. "Please don't leave."

16

HE WAS LOSING her. Panic surged through him. Without thinking, he closed the gap between them and grabbed for her. Anything to keep her here this time. Anything to make her listen. To believe.

Behind him, Gage surged to his feet. He and Lexi's brother had come to an unsteady truce, but he knew one wrong move would have those heavy fists swinging straight for his head.

"Let me go," she whispered, refusing to look up at him.

"No, Lexi. I won't let you go this time. You're too important to me."

She finally looked at him and the expression in her eyes was a punch straight to the gut.

"So important you came into town and didn't even let me know you were here."

He swore beneath his breath. "I didn't think you wanted to see me. I was hoping after you heard about the resort everything would change."

"Why would it?"

His fingers tightened around her arms. He saw

her slight wince and wanted to ease up, but couldn't. "Woman, you would try the patience of a saint. Because I did it for you. I bought the land for you."

"You bought the land because it was a sound investment and you have the skills to make it hugely profitable."

His teeth clicked together with a snap that echoed through the room. Everyone around them had gone perfectly silent, hanging on every word of their exchange.

Beside them, something shifted and caught his eye. His gaze darted sideways long enough to notice Mrs. Copeland smirking a bit gleefully at them.

Without taking his gaze from Lexi's, Brett hollered behind him, "Mr. Harper, I'd like to sign the land over to the town. Do you think the council would approve paying me a dollar?"

Several people gasped and shifted uncomfortably on their chairs.

Lexi's eyes widened. Her father responded, "The council might, but I won't. Son, I won't let you do something that stupid."

"Fine. Anyone else like to take me up on the offer?"

No one answered, but then they didn't have to.

Hope unfurled deep inside Lexi's eyes, crowding out the fear and hesitation.

"Don't," she said, barely audible.

"What?"

"Don't," she said again, this time loud enough for everyone around them to hear. "Don't you dare, Brett Newcomb."

"Does that mean you believe me when I say I don't

care what happens to the land or the resort? The only thing I care about is you. Lexi Harper, I love you."

Her eyes widened and her lips trembled.

"You and this little town you call home. I want to build this resort because I think it's a great project. I think it'll succeed and I think Sweetheart needs something like this. But I can't—won't—do it without you."

Her eyes shimmered with unshed tears, magnifying the vulnerability she tried so hard to hide. The combination nearly brought him to his knees. He hated that he'd hurt her, adding to the harsh lessons she'd already learned.

Wrapping his hand in her hair, he pulled her close. His forehead touched hers and he whispered, "I'm so sorry, Lexi. I didn't mean to hurt you. I promise I'll do my best to never do it again. If you'll give me the chance."

She stared straight into him. He stilled, holding nothing back and hoping she could see the truth behind his words. And waited.

Slowly, hope, love and the flickering flame of need flared deep inside her beautiful chocolate eyes.

"I love you, too," she finally breathed out, the words caressing his face. "I was miserable when you left. I've spent most of my life worrying about what I was doing wrong. From the first moment I met you, you felt right. This feels right."

Her palms bracketed his face. She shifted, bringing their mouths together in a soft kiss. The warm press of her lips was perfect, and yet it wasn't enough. Two weeks was a long time to go without touching her.

Brett crushed her to him and deepened the kiss, uncaring that the entire town watched. He asked her to open to him, pouring every ounce of shaky euphoria and need into the moment so that she could feel and taste just how much she mattered to him.

Several people sighed. A loud harrumph followed by a sour voice ruined the moment. "Y'all should be ashamed. Get a room."

Lexi squirmed in his arms. He could already see the angry rush of embarrassment flaming up her skin. And it pissed him off. Breaking away, Brett kept his arm firmly around Lexi's waist and glared across several heads at Mrs. Copeland.

"After we ruined Mrs. McKinnon's spread, I don't think she'll give us one."

"You got that right," she interjected, her normally surly voice tinged with humor.

Several people around them laughed, but Brett wasn't content to let Mrs. McKinnon's comment defuse the situation.

"If you ever speak to Lexi that way again, Mrs. Copeland, you'll have me to deal with. For someone who teaches etiquette you know nothing about being polite."

A smattering of applause rippled through the crowd.

But he wasn't content with that either. Instead, he picked up where Mrs. Copeland's rudeness had interrupted them.

To hell with the prying eyes; he didn't care about them. As long as he had Lexi in his arms.

He bent to kiss her again, half expecting her to protest. Instead, she surprised him, leaping up into his arms and wrapping her body tightly around his. Her legs locked behind his thighs and her arms circled his neck.

She felt so good.

She met him measure for measure, diving into the kiss just as completely as he did. It swamped them both, blocking out everything but each other.

The entire town thought she was so sweet. And she was, as sweet as anything she sold in her shop. Only he knew Lexi Harper was no angel. But that was okay. He much preferred her apron to a halo.

* * * * *

COMING NEXT MONTH FROM

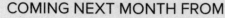 

Available July 23, 2013

#759 THE HEART WON'T LIE • *Sons of Chance*
by Vicki Lewis Thompson

Western writer Michael James Hartford needs to learn how to act like a cowboy—fast. But it isn't until he comes to the Last Chance Ranch—and falls for socialite-turned-housekeeper Keri Fitzgerald—that he really discovers how to ride....

#760 TO THE LIMIT • *Uniformly Hot!*
by Jo Leigh

Air force pilot Sam Brody has had his wings clipped. Now he's only teaching other flyboys. And his fling with the hottest woman on the base has taken a nosedive, too...because Emma Lockwood belongs to someone else.

#761 HALF-HITCHED • *The Wrong Bed*
by Isabel Sharpe

Attending a destination wedding is the *perfect* time for Addie Sewell to seduce Kevin, The One Who Got Away. But when she climbs into the wrong bed and discovers sexy yacht owner Derek, The One Who's Here Right Now might just be the ticket!

#762 TAKING HIM DOWN
by Meg Maguire

Rising MMA star Rich Estrada loves exactly two things—his family and a good scrap. But when sexy Lindsey Tuttle works her way into his heart, keeping his priorities straight may just prove the toughest fight of his life.

YOU CAN FIND MORE INFORMATION ON UPCOMING HARLEQUIN® TITLES, FREE EXCERPTS AND MORE AT WWW.HARLEQUIN.COM.

HBCNM0713

SPECIAL EXCERPT FROM

Enjoy this sneak peek at

Half-Hitched

by Isabel Sharpe, part of The Wrong Bed series
from Harlequin Blaze

Available July 23 wherever
Harlequin books are sold.

Addie Sewell held her breath as she headed for Kevin's room. *First bedroom on the right.*

Eleven years later, she'd feel that wonderful mouth on hers again, would feel those strong arms around her, would feel his hand on her breast. And so much more.

Addie reached for the handle and slipped into the room.

Done!

She closed the door carefully behind her, listening for any sign that Kevin had heard her.

He was still, his breathing slow and even.

She was in.

For a few seconds Addie stood quietly, amazed that she'd actually done this, that she, Princess Rut, had snuck mostly naked into a man's room in order to seduce him.

A sudden calm came over her, This was right.

As silently as possible, she walked toward the bed. In the dim light she could see a swathe of naked back, his head bent, partly hidden by the pillow.

A rush of tenderness. Kevin Ames. The One That Got Away.

She let her sweater pool at her feet as she pictured Kevin hours earlier. Laughing with that Derek Bates and all the other wedding guests.

Totally naked now, heart pounding, she climbed onto the bed then slid down to spoon behind him. His body was warm against hers, his skin soft, his torso much broader than she'd expected. They fit together perfectly.

She knew the instant he woke up, when his body tensed beside hers.

"It's Addie."

"Addie," he whispered.

Addie smiled. She would have thought after all he had to drink and how soundly he'd been passed out downstairs, that she might have trouble waking him.

She drew her fingers down his powerful arm—strangely bigger than she expected. "Do you mind that I'm here?"

He chuckled, deep and low. Addie stilled. She'd *never* heard Kevin laugh like that.

Before she could think further, his body heaved over and she was underneath him, his broad masculine frame trapping her against the sheets. And before she could say anything, he kissed her, a long, slow sweet kiss.

When he came up for air, she knew she'd have to do something. *Say something.*

But then he was kissing her again. And this time her body caught fire.

Because it was so, so good.

Beyond good. Unbelievably good.

It just wasn't Kevin.

Pick up HALF-HITCHED by Isabel Sharpe, available July 23 wherever you buy Harlequin® Blaze® books.

Copyright © 2013 by Muna Shehadi Sill

HBEXP79765

REQUEST YOUR FREE BOOKS!
2 FREE NOVELS PLUS 2 FREE GIFTS!

red-hot reads!

YES! Please send me 2 FREE Harlequin® Blaze™ novels and my 2 FREE gifts (gifts are worth about $10). After receiving them, if I don't wish to receive any more books, I can return the shipping statement marked "cancel." If I don't cancel, I will receive 4 brand-new novels every month and be billed just $4.74 per book in the U.S. or $4.96 per book in Canada. That's a savings of at least 14% off the cover price. It's quite a bargain. Shipping and handling is just 50¢ per book in the U.S. and 75¢ per book in Canada.* I understand that accepting the 2 free books and gifts places me under no obligation to buy anything. I can always return a shipment and cancel at any time. Even if I never buy another book, the two free books and gifts are mine to keep forever.

150/350 HDN F4WC

Name _____ (PLEASE PRINT) _____

Address _____ Apt. # _____

City _____ State/Prov. _____ Zip/Postal Code _____

Signature (if under 18, a parent or guardian must sign) _____

Mail to the **Harlequin®** Reader Service:
IN U.S.A.: P.O. Box 1867, Buffalo, NY 14240-1867
IN CANADA: P.O. Box 609, Fort Erie, Ontario L2A 5X3

Want to try two free books from another line?
Call 1-800-873-8635 or visit www.ReaderService.com.

* Terms and prices subject to change without notice. Prices do not include applicable taxes. Sales tax applicable in N.Y. Canadian residents will be charged applicable taxes. Offer not valid in Quebec. This offer is limited to one order per household. Not valid for current subscribers to Harlequin Blaze books. All orders subject to credit approval. Credit or debit balances in a customer's account(s) may be offset by any other outstanding balance owed by or to the customer. Please allow 4 to 6 weeks for delivery. Offer available while quantities last.

Your Privacy—The Harlequin® Reader Service is committed to protecting your privacy. Our Privacy Policy is available online at www.ReaderService.com or upon request from the Harlequin Reader Service.

We make a portion of our mailing list available to reputable third parties that offer products we believe may interest you. If you prefer that we not exchange your name with third parties, or if you wish to clarify or modify your communication preferences, please visit us at www.ReaderService.com/consumerschoice or write to us at Harlequin Reader Service Preference Service, P.O. Box 9062, Buffalo, NY 14269. Include your complete name and address.

HB13R2

This time, it's no-holds-barred!

Matchmaker Lindsey Tuttle always thought Rich Estrada was a whole lot of sexy. What's not to lust after? He's a gorgeous, flirty mixed martial arts fighter. When they find themselves heating up during an unexpected—and superintense—make-out session, Lindsey is ready...until Rich ends it with no explanation.

Almost a year later, with a broken foot, Rich is back in Boston before his next fight. But this could be the perfect time for a rematch with his sexy little matchmaker....

Pick up

Taking Him Down

by *Meg Maguire*

available July 23, 2013, wherever you buy Harlequin Blaze books.

HARLEQUIN®

Blaze®

Red-Hot Reads
www.Harlequin.com

HB79766

SADDLE UP AND READ 'EM!

Looking for another great Western read? Check out these August reads from the PASSION category!

CANYON by Brenda Jackson
The Westmorelands
Harlequin Desire

THE HEART WON'T LIE by Vicki Lewis Thompson
Sons of Chance
Harlequin Blaze

*Look for these great Western reads AND MORE
available wherever books are sold or visit*
www.Harlequin.com/Westerns

SUART0813PASSION

Boundaries are for breaking...

Air force pilot Sam Brody's posting at Holloman AFB
is a new start...and a brutal reminder that he'll never fly
again. *The bright side?* It's the same town as teacher (and
widow) Emma Lockwood—the woman he's always had a
major thing for. The woman who married his best friend....

Emma doesn't want another hotshot flyboy, no matter
how ridiculously sexy. But with every night of wicked
passion with Sam, she finds herself closer to the point
of no return....

Pick up

To The Limit

by *Jo Leigh*

available July 23, 2013, wherever you buy
Harlequin Blaze books.

HARLEQUIN®

Blaze®

Red-Hot Reads
www.Harlequin.com

HB79764